This month, in
PRETENDING WITH THE PLAYBOY
by Cathleen Galitz,

Meet Alexander Kent—irredeemable playboy,
ladies' man and *husband?* His undercover sting
operation required a wife, and prim librarian
Stephanie Firth was perfect for the part…until he
started involving his heart for real!

**SILHOUETTE DESIRE
IS PROUD TO PRESENT THE**

**TEXAS
Cattleman's Club**

The Stolen Baby

**Six wealthy Texas bachelors—all members of the
state's most exclusive club—must unravel the
mystery surrounding one tiny baby…and
discover true love in the process!**

* * *

**And don't miss
FIT FOR A SHEIKH
by Kristi Gold;
The sixth installment of the**
Texas Cattleman's Club: The Stolen Baby **series.**

Available next month in Silhouette Desire!

Dear Reader,

Thanks so much for choosing Silhouette Desire—*the* destination for powerful, passionate and provocative love stories. Things start heating up this month with Katherine Garbera's *Sin City Wedding*, the next installment of our DYNASTIES: THE DANFORTHS series. An affair, a secret child, a quickie Las Vegas wedding…and that's just the beginning of this romantic tale.

Also this month we have the marvelous Dixie Browning with her steamy *Driven to Distraction*. Cathleen Galitz brings us another book in the TEXAS CATTLEMAN'S CLUB: THE STOLEN BABY series with *Pretending with the Playboy*. Susan Crosby's BEHIND CLOSED DOORS miniseries continues with the superhot *Private Indiscretions*. And Bronwyn Jameson takes us to Australia in *A Tempting Engagement*.

Finally, welcome the fabulous Roxanne St. Claire to the Silhouette Desire family. We're positive you'll enjoy *Like a Hurricane* and will be wanting the other McGrath brothers' stories. We'll be bringing them to you in the months to come as well as stories from Beverly Barton, Ann Major and *New York Times* bestselling author Lisa Jackson. So keep coming back for more from Silhouette Desire.

More passion to you!

Melissa Jeglinski

Melissa Jeglinski
Senior Editor
Silhouette Desire

Please address questions and book requests to:
Silhouette Reader Service
U.S.: 3010 Walden Ave., P.O. Box 1325, Buffalo, NY 14269
Canadian: P.O. Box 609, Fort Erie, Ont. L2A 5X3

Pretending with
the Playboy

CATHLEEN GALITZ

Published by Silhouette Books
America's Publisher of Contemporary Romance

Special thanks and acknowledgment are given
to Cathleen Galitz for her contribution to the
TEXAS CATTLEMAN'S CLUB series.

To Shawn and Curt. Writing this book reminded me
all over again what a precious gift my children are.

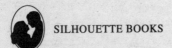

SILHOUETTE BOOKS

ISBN 0-373-76569-X

PRETENDING WITH THE PLAYBOY

Books by Cathleen Galitz

Silhouette Desire

The Cowboy Takes a Bride #1271
Wyoming Cinderella #1373
Her Boss's Baby #1396
Tall, Dark...and Framed? #1433
Warrior in Her Bed #1506
Pretending with the Playboy #1569

Silhouette Romance

The Cowboy Who Broke the Mold #1257
100% Pure Cowboy #1279
Wyoming Born & Bred #1381

CATHLEEN GALITZ,

a Wyoming native, teaches English to students in grades six to twelve in a rural school that houses kindergartners and seniors in the same building. She feels blessed to have married a man who is both supportive and patient. When she's not busy writing, teaching or chauffeuring her sons to and from various activities, she can most likely be found indulging in her favorite pastime—reading.

"What's Happening in Royal?"

NEWS FLASH, March—The most eligible bachelor and stalwart playboy in Royal—tamed? Yes, ladies, break out your handkerchiefs and sob your hearts out—it looks as though Alexander Kent is getting his studly self hitched! Even more shocking is that the lovely wife-to-be is none other than the town's prim librarian, Stephanie Firth. How did a playboy like Alex fall for a gal as steady and proper as Stephanie? Guess the old saying really does apply: Opposites attract...

In other news, we can thank our lucky stars that Dr. Nathan Beldon, aka Birkenfeld, is now firmly behind bars and Carrie Whelan is safely in the embrace of Ry Evans! It's a good thing Ry and Carrie finally came to their senses! But all's not happily ever after just yet; even though Birkenfeld may be in jail, there's a rumor that the black-market adoption ring is still dangerously active....

Come to think of it, Texas Cattleman's Club has been having an awful lot of covert meetings lately. What could those sexy gents be planning? Whatever it is, Alex and Stephanie seem to be in the thick of it....

Prologue

————

"Sorry, guys, no can do," Alexander Kent informed his fellow members of the prestigious Texas Cattleman's Club. ·

His voice lacked any genuine remorse at having to decline the "honor" thrust upon him. Protests arose from every corner of the ultramanly cigar lounge that served as the day's meeting room. Clint Andover, the most recently married among their ranks, succinctly phrased the question on everyone's mind in a warm drawl that belied the steely intent behind the inquiry.

"And just why the hell not?"

Alex studied the fine bone china cup that held his Irish coffee. The club emblem embossed in delicate gold strokes upon the porcelain stood for far more than any outsider could be expected to understand. The facade of their good old boys club was in fact a front for an organization of ex-military men dedicated to saving innocent lives and bringing the guilty to justice. And while their generosity to charities was renowned, it was their covert operations that truly testified to their members' integrity and to the success of their missions.

Alex took his sweet time answering. His gaze swept the room, taking in the exotic animal mounts decorating the walls. He felt a sudden stirring of empathy for the mountain lion trapped for posterity upon a narrow rock jutting out from the opposite wall. Swatting at an imaginary foe, the poor creature's snarl challenged the terrified look in its glassy eyes.

Alex imagined the unfortunate beast had just learned his friends had proposed marrying him off as part of some elaborate plan they had concocted on his behalf.

Overhead a Tiffany chandelier cast a rainbow of prisms upon the club motto hanging from a plaque above the door. The words were carved upon Alex's heart as surely as they were burned into that hallowed piece of wood.

Leadership, Justice and Peace.

It wasn't lack of courage keeping Alex from freely offering himself up as a pawn in the Club's latest mission. They intended to break apart a ring of white-collar criminals engaged in a reprehensible adoption scam. The scam had started coming to light on the fateful day when Natalie Perez stumbled into this proverbial fortress with Travis Whelan's baby—and absolutely no memory whatsoever. Piecing together her recollections had not been easy, or altogether safe, for those who had reached out to help her. And foiling a scheme worth half a million dollars to the perpetrators had proven more perilous than any of them could have imagined at the time.

The fact that Natalie, Travis and their baby were presently out of harm's way, not to mention happily joined together as a bona fide family, wasn't the end of the Cattleman's involvement in this complicated case. Motivated by their pledge to see justice done, the members had seen fit to elect someone to go undercover and conduct a sting operation designed to put an end to the illegal ring for good. Because of his former FBI experience, Alex was the obvious choice for the assignment. Independently wealthy, this single thirty-five-year-old lifetime bachelor had no family or job obligations to prevent him from accepting.

"We're waiting for your answer with bated breath," said Ryan Evans laconically.

Alex gave the former rodeo star a reluctant smile.

"As honored as I am by your faith in me, there's one problem you all seem to have overlooked."

He hesitated. The temptation to crack a joke and charm his way out of this predicament was superceded by his need to be forthright. Alexander Kent could no more lie to the reflection in his own mirror than to the band of brothers who filled this room with the integrity of their own personal character. Taking a deep breath, he removed the invisible mask of indifference that he donned for the rest of the world to see, and prepared himself to be razzed unmercifully.

A rare glimpse of weariness showed itself in his deep green eyes as he made his disclosure.

"In order to play the doting husband in this little scheme of yours, I'm going to need a suitable wife, and the truth is, I'm fresh out of feminine companions who would be willing to act the part—even for as good a cause as this one."

Disbelief and laughter filled the room at the thought of the state's most notorious playboy being unable to cajole any number of women into playing house with him.

"What happened to Glorious Gloria?" someone asked from the back of the room.

"Not speaking to me at the moment," Alex explained in reference to the supermodel who had recently severed ties when he refused to so much as discuss the subject of marriage. "As, I'm afraid, is every other woman in my infamous little black book."

The one that doesn't exist, he silently amended.

His friends' good-natured kidding didn't do anything to ease the loneliness that he secretly dealt with every day as part of his inheritance from a wealthy father who had been taken by any number of rapacious stepmothers. Very early on, those women had taught young Alex how to appreciate the value of bachelorhood. Gloria Vuu was the latest in the long line of women frustrated in an attempt to get him to commit to something beyond what she called his "swinging singles' mind-set." Her dramatic departure had included the breaking of a priceless vase against a wall of his penthouse. Never one to quibble over the price of splitting up, Alex was just grateful she hadn't been a better aim.

"That one wouldn't have worked for our purposes anyway," interjected another friendly voice. "Nobody in their right mind would believe somebody like Gloria was desperate to saddle herself to a pile of dirty diapers."

With his usual aplomb, Ryan Evans quieted the room simply by clearing his throat. "Is that all that's keeping you from accepting this assignment?" he asked, spearing Alex with a searching look.

As if that wasn't enough!

Alex nodded. Just because his bachelor friends were dropping like flies into the honeyed web of matrimony, he hardly thought it fair that they suddenly considered themselves experts on who would make him a suitable wife.

"If that's the case, I'm one step ahead of you, partner," Ryan said with typical brashness.

The Cheshire grin his friend wore worried Alex.

As if afraid of being interrupted, Ryan continued in a rush. "Since it's a given that none of the ladies you usually hang out with would provide you with a believable cover, I took the liberty of asking Carrie if she could think of someone who might fit the part. It just so happens that she has a friend who would be perfect marriage material for you."

Alex was just about to ask exactly what he meant by that, when Travis interrupted his soon-to-be-brother-in-law and longtime buddy. "If my little sister gives the lady the thumbs-up, that's good enough for me."

The set of his chiseled jaw dared anyone to question his judgment on the matter. Since Carrie had at one time been romantically involved with the doctor suspected of heading up this nefarious ring and who later turned on her with diabolical vengeance, there was no need to brief her on the need for utmost secrecy in regard to their plan. With both Travis and Ryan giving the mystery woman Carrie had picked out for him their seal of approval, no one else saw any reason to argue. Alex was morbidly curious to see just who Ry thought was the firecracker of a fiancée that would make him the perfect mate. If she was even half as pretty as Carrie, he knew he'd have a heck of a time staying focused on the business at hand.

The thought perked him up considerably.

"And just *who* might that be?" he wanted to know, mentally running through a list of available single women in town and crossing each and every one off as he came to them.

The name Ryan supplied had him picking his jaw up off the floor.

"The school librarian?" Alex asked in disbelief.

"One and the same. Before you object, you need to know that the lady not only has all the right understated qualities needed to actually pull this off, she's also got some acting experience under her belt."

Her chastity belt you mean, Alex was tempted to add.

Quite frankly he was offended that Carrie would pick such a dowdy old maid as his "perfect" match. Not that Alex was one to fault a woman for living virtuously. If his own mother had shown more restraint than an alley cat before up and leaving her husband and five-year-old son high and dry, maybe he wouldn't be as emotionally screwed up as Gloria and an entire string of scorned women claimed he was.

On second thought, there were certain advantages to having such a plain Jane cast as his make-believe wife for this mission. Such a woman wasn't likely to come on board this project with any preconceived notions about becoming romantically attached to him, which would make it a whole lot easier for him to keep his focus. When dealing with dangerous criminals, the less distractions the better. As much as he would like to consider this assignment a lark, Alex understood just how perilous the game was they were playing. A man who would stoop to stealing babies from vulnerable single mothers wasn't likely to balk at murder.

Alex couldn't imagine the mild-mannered woman he had met at local school fund–raisers as being up to such a challenge. He doubted whether the demure Stephanie Firth would be willing to risk her precious reputation for a good cause, let alone actually risk her neck by placing herself in the kind of compromising situations demanded by the plan Alex's friends had concocted.

Whatever threat such a plan posed to him personally, Alex would not turn his back on everything he held dear. The pledge he had taken as a Texas Cattleman precluded his ever saying no to the friends who'd placed their trust in him. The thought of decent women like Natalie grieving for the babies they believed to be dead at birth demanded nothing less than laying his own life on the line if necessary.

Looking around the room at all the expectant faces turned toward him, Alex threw up his hands in surrender and put the onus on Miss Prim herself.

"All right, guys, if you think there's a chance in hell of convincing the little lady to go along with this, you're welcome to count me in."

One

"**R**omeo, Romeo, wherefore art thou, Romeo?" asked a blond Juliet with an impatient hand planted upon her hip.

"Probably in the wings making out with my nurse," she added under her breath before crying out in a shrill voice, "Miss Firth, won't you do *something* about the way Junior keeps missing his cues?"

Stephanie bit the inside of her cheek to keep the expletive ricocheting inside her brain from exploding out her mouth. Shakespeare would flip over in his grave and pack his ears with dirt to keep from hearing the Royal, Texas, version of his greatest love story. Taking a deep breath, she reminded herself that the cast comprised high-school students and, as such, could not be expected to put on a Broadway production. Nevertheless, Stephanie had little desire to be publicly humiliated by a performance straight out of Dog Patch. Indeed, one could almost hear "y'all" dripping off the end of every single line spoken during today's rehearsal.

In responding to Juliet's petulance, the voice Stephanie employed to get her message across was that of a disciplined school employee used to working with hormonally charged adolescents.

"Launa Beth, how many times must I remind you to stay in character, and let me worry about the other cast members? Now, I want you to really focus on softening your accent in this scene."

Unhappy at being chastised when Junior Weaver was the one so sorely in need of upbraiding, Launa squinted into the darkened theater. She was distracted from her prima-donna bout of peevishness by Romeo's belated entrance. An athletic young man sauntered on stage looking more like a lost football player than a love-struck leading man.

Furious, Juliet hurled at him the insult most fashionable among her peers. "Junior, you suck!"

Turning an irresistible smile upon her, Romeo corrected her in true Elizabethan fashion. "Don't you mean sucketh, milady?"

"Cut!"

Stephanie's voice echoed throughout the theater, drowning out the stifled laughter of an unannounced visitor sitting in the back. Unbeknownst to her, this particular patron of the arts was not there to watch the production but rather to scope out the harried director herself. Had Stephanie realized that she was auditioning for the role of a lifetime, she likely would have felt more self-conscious as she marched up on-stage and proceeded to instruct her students in the finer art of acting.

Absorbed in the scene unfolding before him, Alexander Kent leaned forward in his seat. He recognized the librarian who was picked to become his make-believe wife by the plain clothes and no-frills hairstyle she favored, but he was surprised by the passion with which she directed her misbegotten cast of characters. The transformation was nothing short of astonishing.

"You have to put your personal feelings aside and truly become your character," Stephanie told the assembled cast as she emerged from the darkness and strode into the limelight herself. "Need I remind you that when you step onto this stage, you are stepping back into time, not only into your character's shoes but rather into the very skin of those who risked everything they had for the sake of love? I'm asking you to find the courage to forget yourself for a brief couple of hours and don the mantle of a real actor."

Lifting a piece of gauze draped around the column of Juliet's balcony, Stephanie wrapped it loosely around her shoulders and assumed a theatrical pose. The bright violet hue of her improvised shawl contrasted sharply with the beige skirt and sweater that she wore. The dull color did little to accentuate her fair complexion. However, her bright eyes flashed with intensity discernible even from Alex's back-row seat.

"As the timeless bard himself so eloquently put

it—'All the world's a stage, and all the men and women merely players. They have their exits and their entrances, and one man in his time plays many parts...'''

Alex was struck by the quality and sincerity of the voice delivering those lines from memory. Had his own high-school teacher taught with such zeal, it was entirely possible that he might have developed an honest appreciation for the great master of thees and thous. As it was, he still blanched at the thought of so much as attending a Shakespearean production, let alone participating in one.

Unaware that her form was being reviewed on multiple levels, Stephanie continued with raw feeling. ''If you dare to dig deep enough inside yourself to speak these immortal lines from the depths of a young star-crossed lover's heart, when you plunge a dagger into your own breast and die for us upon this very stage—''

Stephanie paused to gesture toward the wooden flooring beneath her feet as if it were indeed hallowed ground. ''If you can manage that, then you can fix Romeo and Juliet's tragic sacrifice like a brilliant meteor streaking across the night sky of your audience's minds and change their perception of the world forever.''

Alex was tempted to applaud. He was stunned to discover that beneath the breast of their mild-mannered school librarian beat the heart of a hopeless romantic. One capable of inspiring a cast of adolescents, not to mention a self-proclaimed playboy who had long ago given up on such a starry-eyed notion as irrefutable true love. Alex couldn't remember the last time he had longed for more than a fleeting liaison to hold his interest. Without her even knowing he was part of an audience, this dowdy librarian turned director made him suddenly wish he wasn't so jaded.

Maybe he'd been wrong about Stephanie Firth. Anybody who could draw him toward the flame of romantic ever-afters like a hapless moth intent on self-immolation might actually stand a chance of convincing some devious criminal that she was willing to pay any price to make her dreams of motherhood come true.

Alex felt a tug upon his elbow.

"Didn't I tell you she was wonderful?" Carrie Whelan whispered in his ear. Her hazel eyes danced with gleaming flames the same color as her hair.

"You don't have to convince me," Alex told his self-appointed emissary in his quest to enlist this woman's help. "The reason that we're here is to see if your friend is willing to put her acting talents to a real-life test."

"Absolutely not!" Stephanie exclaimed, shaking her head as if to clear her ears of a painful obstruction.

She couldn't believe that her friend had actually broached the subject of her faking a marriage with the most infamous playboy in all of Texas. Scanning the area for hidden cameras, she wondered if her reaction was being broadcast on one of those practical-joke reality shows that she hated. In her opinion, the pranks tended to be more mean-spirited than funny.

This one was no exception. If Carrie had endured that awful rehearsal just to get Alexander Kent up on stage with her, Stephanie had to wonder at their friendship. It felt like a horrible practical joke. She hated to even consider the possibility.

Stephanie's dismay was evident in her dark brown eyes that widened just enough to allow Alex to sample their chocolaty depths. He was as surprised by her antagonism as by how lovely those eyes were without the aid of cosmetics. The women he usually spent time with wouldn't be caught dead without their makeup meticulously—if not professionally—applied. Flecks of gold dust shimmered in the dark irises of Stephanie's eyes. Velvet-brown dark curtains that briefly opened in surprise to reveal a soul untouched by evil snapped shut again with a blink of naturally long eyelashes.

Hoping that humor would be a good strategy to ease the tension, Alex fell back on his characteristic charm.

"In certain quarters," he said, "women have been known to leap at the chance of having me as their husband, albeit prematurely."

"Would that be in the French Quarter?" Stephanie demanded. She was clearly not in the least impressed with the opportunity to join the ranks of those women.

Carrie snorted indelicately.

When Alex had the audacity to look hurt, Stephanie refused to feel any empathy for him. If Alexander Kent was expecting to win her over with the kind of superficial charisma that had every other woman in Royal panting over him, he had another long, hard think coming. Had he asked exactly why she seemed to take such an immediate dislike to him, Stephanie would have been forced to admit that it had less to do with his effect upon women and more with the fact that he had never given her as much as a passing glance. She could never hope to be included in this man's circle of rich and beautiful friends. That didn't bother her nearly as much as the fact that he made her so acutely aware of her shortcomings in terms of standards of beauty set forth in women's magazines— the same magazines in which his latest girlfriend could surely be found modeling this year's skimpiest swimwear.

A case in point was the last school fund-raiser in which she and Alex had been thrown into contact. Not that she expected Alex to recall the incident. Carrie had coerced Stephanie into volunteering her creative talents at the poetry booth where, for a simple donation, Stephanie had penned original poems for customers on any topic of their choice. Carrie had put her friend's words into calligraphy and wrapped the masterpiece in a delicate, ribboned scroll. As ingenious as their efforts had been, the adjoining stand took away most of their business.

Stephanie had been flabbergasted when sexy playboy Alexander Kent waltzed into the kissing booth and proceeded to make as much money as the other booths put together. Carrie's flippant offer to buy her a much needed kiss from that scoundrel vividly stuck in her mind—perhaps as much for her angry protests that she wasn't *that* desperate as by the fact that she had secretly been tempted to take Carrie up on her

offer. Alexander, however, had been so busy puck-
ering up for the seemingly endless line of Royal's
single women stretching across the gym floor that he
hadn't so much as noticed Stephanie's presence.

Now that "Hot Lips" Kent suddenly needed her to
play a part in some ridiculous game, he thought all
he had to do was turn on that notorious smile and she
would melt like a strawberry ice-cream cone on a hot
summer's day.

Fat chance.

Just because she wasn't the loveliest swan in the
lake didn't mean this ugly duckling didn't have her
pride.

"Look, Steph," Carrie interjected before Alex had
the chance to defend himself. "You have to know
that I wouldn't ask if it wasn't for a good cause.
Please just hear us out before making your decision."

Suspecting that *she* was the "good cause", Stephanie worried that Carrie was up to her old matchmaking tricks once again. Granted, this veritable
Adonis was a far cry from the last uninspired blind
date that Carrie had thrust upon her, but at least that
date hadn't made her feel like a charity case. Then
again, that pleasant but uninteresting man hadn't had
the effect on her senses that Don Juan here did. Her
body betrayed common sense as her pulse leaped in
feminine awareness of Alexander's nearness and she
turned her ire upon the source of her distress.

"If Mr. Kent needs a piece of eye candy to dangle
off his arm for some amusing spot of entertainment,
I hardly think he's in the right shop," Stephanie said
primly.

She was determined not to let anyone beat her to a punch line about her personal appearance.

Alex tested his weight against one of the pillars holding up Juliet's balcony and found it surprisingly sturdy. He picked up her cue like a true professional and drawled, "With a disposition as sweet as yours, I can't imagine how you could possibly categorize yourself as being sugar free."

They glared at each other. As if she feared what such verbal sparring could lead to, Carrie held up both hands in a classic crossing-guard pose.

"This is no game," Carrie assured Stephanie. "It's about helping unsuspecting women like my future sister-in-law who were tricked into believing that their babies died at birth so some monster parading as a doctor could make it rich selling them to the highest bidder."

Stephanie's gasp echoed her sense of outrage. Everyone in town knew about how a wild-eyed, disheveled woman by the name of Natalie Perez stumbled into the Royal Diner a few short months ago with a baby in her arms, but only a select few were privy to the real story behind her amnesia. Any overt speculation had been stifled by the fact that she had recently married Carrie's overly protective and notoriously hot-tempered brother. Now Carrie proceeded to relate the seedier aspects of Natalie's harrowing tale, and Stephanie found herself wiping away tears blurring her vision.

Upon delivering a baby girl, Natalie had been told by her boss, who also just happened to be her doctor, that her infant had died at birth. Natalie had discovered that Birkenfeld had hired other pregnant single mothers in the past to work for him—and that an abnormal percentage of them also lost their babies at birth or shortly thereafter. Further investigation led her to find a partial list of birth certificates corresponding to the supposed deaths.

When her own baby was stolen, through an amazing set of circumstances, she was able to steal the infant back—as well as a sizable amount of cash used to fund such operations. Realizing that she would have to involve the baby's unwitting father in the whole sordid mess if she hoped to ever offer their child a normal life, she sought him out by means of a Texas Cattleman's Club card that he had given her when they had parted, insisting she call him if she ever needed his help.

Carrie had confided that her brother, Travis, was the child's biological father and that he had officially accepted responsibility for the baby and her mother the day they were wed. Stephanie could certainly understand why Natalie wouldn't want to involve herself any further in this investigation until the perpetrators of this heinous crime were behind bars. And why she still worried about her baby's safety.

Carrie admitted that Natalie still suffered nightmares in which the criminals whom she'd thwarted pursued her relentlessly, intent on recovering the money she had ''stolen'' from them and exacting their revenge upon her. At the present time, the most Natalie could do without further endangering herself and her baby was to point the Cattlemen in the direction of the private adoption agency in Las Vegas that had shown up so frequently in Birkenfeld's mail while she was working for him.

Stephanie knew little about the exclusive Texas Cattleman's Club other than what she'd read in newspaper accounts of their glittering off-limits parties. What Alex proceeded to tell her in strictest confidence came as a tremendous shock to her. It seemed that the Club was actually a front for the wealthiest men in the state to work covertly on secret missions to save lives. It was even more unbelievable to think that Alexander Kent was a part of such a courageous organization. The idea that he might be using his playboy image as subterfuge to hide such a secret was hard to swallow.

Stephanie had always held that stuffy old boys club in contempt. Despite the charitable contributions the Cattleman's Club made to innumerable worthy causes, she couldn't help turning a resentful eye to an organization that made such a point of excluding everyone but the most privileged from their ranks. Still, Stephanie was moved by the tragic story. Romeo and Juliet had nothing on Natalie Perez. Having always secretly longed for a child of her own, the thought of someone stealing an infant for monetary gain made her sick to her stomach.

"Can we count on you?" Carrie asked.

Her friend's trust weighed heavily upon Stephanie. To be honored with such highly confidential knowledge of the Texas Cattleman's Club's clandestine operations was in itself a rare honor. Not to mention that a person would have to have a heart of stone not to want to help such unfortunate young women and their poor babies. Carrie knew full well that one of Stephanie's greatest faults was that her heart was too tender for her own good.

Still, she had her reputation to consider. As a school employee and role model for the young people with whom she worked, Stephanie could hardly go gallivanting around the country over spring break posing as a married woman with one of the most notorious playboys in the state and expect to have a job waiting for her when she returned. Nor did she relish the thought of people laughing behind her back at the news that the most eligible bachelor in all of Texas had settled for someone generally considered as dull and conservative as their local school librarian. No doubt, many would leap to the assumption that pregnancy played a hand in this hasty marriage.

At thirty-one, she may have given up any illusions about ever being cast as an ingenue in a real-life role, but the idea of playing the part of the comic foil to Alexander's handsome hero wasn't exactly appealing either. Having spent a goodly portion of her adult life doing everything within her power to keep from being openly laughed at, as she had been during her public-school days, she hesitated to commit to this plan.

"I'm n-not sure," she stammered.

"So I guess all that pontificating onstage about putting aside one's personal feelings for the good of the cause was nothing more than an act designed to manipulate naive teenagers who don't know any better than to trust anyone the school board hires. Apparently you don't buy into any of it yourself." Sensing her wavering commitment, Alex couldn't refrain from goading her. He had been there the night that Natalie had stumbled into the Royal Diner, and he would never forget the terrified look on her face before she collapsed. And the idea that this uptight little book-worm considered herself too good for him was a blow to his sense of masculine pride. He was quick to hold up a mirror so she could take a good look at herself.

Stephanie bristled.

"Who are you to judge me?" she snapped. "You don't have a clue who I am or what I stand for. Yet you have the gall to stand there in your expensive Italian loafers and mock me."

The fire in those deceptive doelike eyes intrigued Alex. He wondered if, like her self-righteous indignation, passion had the power to stir those fascinating embers to life.

"One could say the same for you," Alex replied. "I would think that as a librarian, Miss Firth, you of all people should know better than to judge a book by its cover."

The old axiom failed to coax a smile from her lips. Stephanie was obviously skeptical of the devil-may-care-rogue front that Alexander used as a member of the Cattleman's Club. It kept anyone from trespassing too closely to his true feelings. That this prim-and-proper librarian brought those repressed feelings to the surface was more than mildly disturbing. Although he had initially been doubtful about involving Stephanie Firth at all, Alex suddenly wanted very much to get to know this woman better, if only to prove to her that he was not the shallow fellow she thought him to be. He sensed that he would have to proceed carefully if he hoped to convince her to join forces with the Texas Cattlemen.

"The only other reason I can think of for you to turn this offer down is that you're worried your own acting skills aren't up to a real-life test. You would rather hide in the wings than to commit to using your own talent."

Turning his eyes upon her like emerald drill bits, Alex moved in for the kill.

"I'm sure you're familiar with the old expression. Those who can, do. Those who can't, teach."

Nothing else he could have possibly said would have had the power to infuriate Stephanie more. Like her colleagues, she was sensitive to such off-base criticism. She would love to see how long Alexander Kent would last in a public school setting. She'd wager a month's salary that the kids would eat his lunch before he could so much as file a single overdue book. They had literally tied up the last substitute drama coach who had filled in for her when she was out with the flu, and left her onstage hollering for help for the better part of an hour.

"If anyone needs to be concerned about their acting abilities, rest assured it is not I, Mr. Kent," Stephanie rejoined in a regal tone. "It's going to take a whole lot more than dashing good looks to convince anyone that you're someone who would want a baby in his life for anything more than a photo opportunity."

Her words cut more deeply than Stephanie could have known. They jolted Alex back to a childhood in which he himself had been used by a number of selfish women as a means of getting their hooks into his all-too-vulnerable father after his mother had deserted them.

"I'm up to the challenge if you are," he said, tossing down the gauntlet with a cocky smile that belied the painful memories flitting through his mind.

By now, Stephanie was so infuriated that she would have strapped herself to a motorcycle and attempted a jump over the Grand Canyon had that been the dare leveled at her.

"You're on, pretty boy," she said, accepting his challenge with the impetuousness of a character in Shakespeare's Verona rather than the demure woman who spent her days cataloging books in a Texas secondary-school library.

"As my wife, don't you think you should call me by my first name, sweetheart?" he purred, gracing her with a smile known to liquefy even the most stubborn ice princess.

"That's not the name that comes to mind," Stephanie muttered under her breath.

Indeed, the endearment ricocheting in her head was one that local censors objected to in any of the books occupying space in their hallowed public-school library.

"Then it's settled," piped up Carrie, whose presence had been forgotten.

Now Carrie clapped her hands together in glee. Despite the fact that Juliet employed no less lethal a dagger than the glare her friend leveled at her, Carrie was delighted with the way things were going.

Whether either of these two wanted to admit it or not, the sexual tension zinging between them only reinforced her belief that she was indeed peerless as Royal's preeminent matchmaker.

Two

"**M**ethinks the lady doth protest too much."

Grinning, Carrie turned the famous bard's words upon Stephanie when she complained of being tricked into participating in an impossible scheme that might very well cost her more than just her self-respect. Clearly, the morning after, Stephanie was having second thoughts. The dollop of cream she stirred into her cup of coffee was liberally laced with doubt.

"How dare you use Shakespeare to advance the cause of your elaborate little matchmaking scheme?" she demanded.

The look of mock innocence that Carrie donned caused Stephanie to roll her eyes. Carrie might believe herself to be sly, but she was as translucent as glass. It would have been laughable had it not been her and had the plan not ultimately proven so effective.

"Oh, come on," Carrie wheedled. "Are you denying that the thought of spending spring break in Vegas as Alexander Kent's bride doesn't excite you just a teeny little bit?"

"Yes, I am," Stephanie affirmed with an indignant sniff. "And I will deny it with my dying breath if I have to."

"You go right on trying to convince yourself, girlfriend, but you're wasting your breath on me."

Ignoring the warning look Stephanie gave her beneath a cocked eyebrow, Carrie continued, "As much allure as the library and this lovely efficiency apartment obviously holds for you, I can't believe you aren't the least intrigued by the thought of venturing into the role of a lifetime with someone as ideal as Alexander Kent."

Taking a sip of caramel-flavored coffee, Carrie paused to sigh. The hedonistic pleasure her sigh suggested made Stephanie wonder how Carrie thought someone as inexperienced as she could convincingly play the part of a woman in love. Especially with someone like Alexander Kent.

"How does your husband-to-be feel about you bestowing the title of Mr. Perfect upon another man?"

"I didn't, the *Texas Tattler* did," Carrie replied. She flipped the newspaper open to the society pages. "It says here that after breaking up with Gloria Vuu, Alexander Kent is back on the market, thereby regaining his standing as the most eligible bachelor in Texas."

"I can hardly wait to see what they'll have to say about this spur-of-the-moment marriage," Stephanie mulled over aloud. She envisioned a headline reading Beauty and the Beast Wed! There was no doubt in her mind who the press would dub as the latter.

Even though Carrie assured Stephanie that she had blossomed into a beautiful woman, she still thought of herself in terms of the gangly class brain from her public-school days. Thick glasses had been replaced by soft contact lenses, but playground taunts of "beanpole" and "egghead" still had the power to make her doubt her very grown-up appeal with the opposite sex.

"They'll say he's lucky to have finally found someone wonderful enough to bring him to his senses—and the editors will be so jealous, their ink will undoubtedly turn green."

Stephanie gave her friend a doubtful look. "People are bound to notice we're not particularly—"

She paused to search for the right word.

"Well suited…"

"Opposites have been known to attract" was Carrie's wry response. "In case you are unaware of it, the heat between the two of you fairly threatened to burn down the theater last night."

"In case you didn't recognize it, *that* was *hostility*," Stephanie explained. She articulated the last word carefully, as if she were speaking to the village idiot.

"Uh-huh."

Carrie's obstinacy was nearly as infuriating as Alexander's attitude.

"Oh, all right!" Stephanie exclaimed, realizing that it was useless to deny the obvious. "I won't bother arguing that the man is drop-dead gorgeous and richer than Croesus."

Carrie's triumphant smile was short-lived.

"He's also arrogant, conceited and shallow."

Her friend looked so surprised at the vehemence of such a proclamation that Stephanie felt compelled to elaborate.

"And he's no more thrilled about having me pretend to be his wife than I am about it. In fact, if the truth were known, I'd wager a month's salary that Alexander Kent's massive ego was hurt something awful at his fellow Cattlemen's suggestion that he drape someone as ordinary and plain as me over his arm for this little charade."

"You are one of the most extraordinary people I know!" Carrie objected with a forcefulness equal to Stephanie's.

"Don't you mean extraordinarily plain?"

The hurt in her big brown eyes would have been enough to make less of a friend shrink from the truth. Carrie used it as an opportunity to advance an issue that she had been harping on for ages.

"No, I don't. But I don't understand why you go to such lengths to hide your looks either. You know it wouldn't hurt you to wear something with a belt once in a while or maybe consider updating your hairstyle. You've worn it that way since high school."

Instinctively, Stephanie's hand reached out to touch her demure coif. "What's wrong with my hair?"

"Nothing that my stylist wouldn't love to—"

A knock on the door interrupted her midthought. Powered by caffeine and a need to escape Carrie's self-improvement spiel, Stephanie bolted from her chair and put an eye up to the standard-issue peephole provided in every door in the apartment complex.

"You won't believe who it is," she hissed over her shoulder.

Carrie chuckled. Grabbing her purse from the back of her chair where she had slung it earlier, she rose to her feet.

"Your husband maybe?"

Hearing nothing but a painful gurgling sound in response, Carrie took a final swallow of her coffee as she stepped around Stephanie, who remained rooted to her spot in the doorway.

"If you have no objections, I'll just leave the two of you honeymooners alone," she said.

"I do object," Stephanie said, but it was too late. Her friend was already in the process of opening the door.

Carrie took her leave with a cheerful greeting to Alex on her way out.

Unlike poor Junior Weaver who had yet to grasp the impact of making a timely dramatic appearance, Alex swept into the room carrying a dozen long-stemmed red roses. He presented them to Stephanie with a flourish. Fragrance and color flooded the tiny living room. His larger-than-life presence made it seem even smaller.

"I hope you haven't packed yet," Alex said, looking around the room. What the place lacked in extravagance, it more than made up for in tidy coziness.

As much as Stephanie wanted to believe she was immune to the attentions of a fine-looking man standing in the middle of her living room proffering blossoms the size of a fist, her body told her otherwise. Her pulse registered his proximity with scientific precision. She felt hot all over. And her heartbeat galloped out of control at the thought that Alexander was here to tell her that he had changed his mind about using her. If she hadn't been so incredibly nervous, that such a thought brought more anguish than relief would have given her reason to pause.

"I haven't so much as started to pack," she said, congratulating herself for having the good sense to resist the urge to do so when she had returned home last night, unable to sleep a wink.

As hard as she tried, Stephanie couldn't get over the feeling that she was being made the butt of some horrible practical joke. She had invited Carrie over for coffee this morning thinking her friend would confirm that gut feeling and own up to her part in the prank. When Carrie had failed to validate that theory, it had been impossible to resist a growing sense of excitement. What woman *wouldn't* be tempted by the prospect of embarking upon a wildly romantic adventure with one of the most sought-after men in all of Texas? An adventure that not only would place her right in the middle of Sin City itself with an entirely new identity, but one that also had the potential to make the world a better, safer place.

"I'm glad to hear it."

Alexander looked pleased that he had arrived in time to spare her the inconvenience of unpacking her meager belongings. Hoping she was a good enough actress to hide her disappointment, Stephanie steeled herself against the let down that he had found some-one better-looking and more socially connected to play the part of his wife.

He bestowed upon her a smile that threatened to melt her bones into a puddle.

"I'd like to take you shopping this morning," he said. "A woman with a new identity along with a new husband needs a new wardrobe, don't you think? The weather in Vegas is bound to be warmer than what it is here, and if we're going to pretend to be married, my wife needs a suitable trousseau."

Stephanie couldn't have been more shocked by Alex if he had just stepped out of her closet wearing nothing but her underwear.

"W-what?" she stammered.

He repeated himself. "Trousseau, new clothes tra-ditionally bought specifically for and worn on one's honeymoon."

"I know what trousseau means," Stephanie snapped. "I just don't think it's necessary to go to such expense."

"Of course it is," Alexander told her confidently. "If only to maintain the illusion."

Speaking of illusions, he hoped to catch a magic show while they were in Vegas. Since Stephanie clearly hadn't bought into their mission one hundred percent, he could use all the professional pointers he could glean from a Siegfried and Roy production if he hoped to pull this off.

Hands upon her hips, Stephanie looked him straight

in the eye. "Are you by any chance implying that my clothes are unacceptable for this undertaking?"

Alexander didn't flinch from the truth.

"In a word, yes."

Stephanie's anger at his response was barely controlled. "Surely you're aware that clothes don't make the actor?"

"And surely you know that costuming is as integral to a theatrical performance as setting the stage beforehand."

The red burgeoning upon Stephanie's cheeks rivaled the roses he had brought her. That traditional prop had failed him miserably. Although Alex hadn't meant to hurt her feelings about her limited wardrobe, she was so damn prickly about every little detail that it was difficult to be tactful.

"Look," he said, running a hand through a thatch of thick dark hair in a gesture of exasperation. "I don't know what I did to get off on the wrong foot with you, but I brought you these flowers as a peace offering. The least you could do is put them in water."

"Thank you," Stephanie added pensively, remembering to respond with the kind of courtesy that her mother would have expected of her. "They're lovely."

The smile that broke through the fog of her bad temper caught Alex by surprise. When she stopped glaring at him long enough to bury her nose in those perfumed blossoms something stirred deep inside him. He couldn't remember how long it had been since any woman had shown such appreciation for a gift as simple as those fleeting crimson petals. They overpowered the diminutive coffee table on which she placed them a moment later.

"Won't you sit down?" she asked him stiffly.

Alex took a seat on a faded but clean couch that he suspected had come as part and parcel of a furnished apartment. He had come by his own money honestly enough, but the thought of this hardworking lady struggling day after day to pull people away from their televisions and hand-held electronic games to discover the joy of reading—and consequently living a lifestyle of scarcity made him feel somehow guilty for the abundance that marked his own life.

"Flowers are one thing," Stephanie said, her gaze lingering upon them for a moment before looking at him directly. "But a whole new wardrobe is something else entirely. There's no way I could accept such an extravagant and intimate gift from any man, even under the guise of purchasing costumes for a good cause. Besides, haven't you ever heard of the folly of trying to turn a sow's ear into a silk purse?"

Alex frowned. Besides not being able to recall a single woman in his past who ever worried about taking advantage of his generosity, he took exception to the self-deprecating remark. Like a wave rushing toward a foreign strand, it caused an unexpected swell of protectiveness to rise inside him. Why Stephanie's old-fashioned scruples made him feel like showering her with gifts was a perplexing paradox.

"If it's the money you're worried about, there's no reason to be. In case I didn't mention the amount that Natalie was carrying when she found us, it's around half a million dollars. The cash is tucked away in a safe down at the Cattleman's Club and at our disposal anytime we need it. Since Natalie claims the money isn't hers and believes that it is, in fact, ill-gotten gains, I doubt very much whether she'd mind us using some of it to protect her baby—and the babies of women who find themselves in similar circumstances.''

Alex saw no reason to tell Stephanie he intended to personally fund their week in Vegas as well as purchase her brand-new wardrobe out of his own petty cash. He had the sneaking suspicion that information would only provide her with a misguided sense of obligation to repay him out of her paltry salary.

''Half a million dollars,'' she repeated in a tone suggesting that amount of money was beyond comprehension. She paused to consider the sum. ''In that case, I suppose it couldn't hurt to pick up a few things—if only to help set the stage like you said.''

Alex's smile was reassuring. It warmed her from the inside out. Suddenly the prospect of going shopping didn't seem so daunting. Stephanie herself would concede that her choice in clothes had more to do with practicality than with any thought of pleasing a man. And that was something a newlywed would be expected to do. She hoped Alex wouldn't ask her to wear some frilly thing that would make her feel uncomfortable. She was used to comfort and affordability. Stephanie couldn't picture herself in some skimpy getup like the ones she saw in the fashion magazines. On the other hand she couldn't imagine walking into a typical discount store with this man, let alone scouring the bargain racks with him at her side.

"I hope you're prepared to raise a few eyebrows," she said, envisioning the commotion just being seen with Alexander Kent was sure to cause.

Stephanie issued the warning entirely for Alex's benefit and was surprised by his reaction: a lusty belly laugh that filled her apartment and lightened her heart.

"I live for it," he assured his wife-to-be.

Having been a constant source of gossip since his mother abandoned him at the tender age of five, Alexander didn't care a fig what anybody had to say behind his back. In fact, he often took perverse delight in confounding the local gossip columnists and rumormongers. However, he couldn't help but give some consideration to the fact that Stephanie's reputation in this conservative community was far more precious to her than his would ever be to him.

"I have an idea," he said conspiratorially, lowering his voice.

Patting the empty seat next to him on the couch, he invited her to sit down and lend him an ear. When Stephanie finally succumbed to the alluring wink that he threw in for good measure, Alex leaned in close enough that she could hear without straining.

"Since we know they're going to talk about this anyway, what do you say we give them something really juicy to chew on?"

The suggestion struck Stephanie so funny that she actually laughed out loud. Alex was caught off guard by the sound of anything so utterly girlish escaping those surprisingly full lips. All too often, women made a point of laughing around him in a calculated effort to ensure that everyone in the vicinity was aware that they were together. The sound of pure amusement, Stephanie's laughter was free of any such disingenuousness. It was also so infectious that he was unable to keep from joining in.

The delicate scent of the perfume that Stephanie wore threatened to undermine the unexpected camaraderie budding between them. Far from the heavy, expensive fragrances his other lady friends had specially mixed at great cost to interact with their own unique body chemistry, Alex was pretty sure this particular brand could easily be picked up off the shelf at any number of stores in the area. If he could coax the brand name from her, he'd have to stop by and pick up a gross or two. The stuff was utterly intoxicating.

Stephanie's eyes sparkled mischievously as she accepted his offer for what it was: an invitation for a day of pure, unadulterated fun.

"I suppose if you really want to go shopping for trouble, you can count me in."

Three

————

Just as Stephanie predicted, trouble was available in a variety of sizes and colors at the most exclusive boutique in town. And just as she feared, Alex refused to step foot in any of the department stores where she usually shopped, insisting that any wife of his might as well start acting the part of a wealthy socialite. The saleslady at the first shop they patronized took one look at Stephanie's workaday jeans and sniffed, giving the distinct impression that a polecat had wandered through the door instead of a bona fide customer. She held a tissue delicately up to her nose.

"May I help you?" she asked.

Momentarily detained on the street by an old friend, Alex watched through the front window as the woman directed Stephanie to a sales rack at the back of the store where she disposed of her customer with an aristocratic sneer. The jaw-dropping looks the sales tags produced upon Stephanie's face didn't do anything to advance her plight with the pretentious clerk.

''Are they out of their minds?'' she gasped, unable to believe the outrageous prices attached to last season's fashions.

''There's a bargain-basement special across the way that you might find more in your price range,'' the clerk informed Stephanie before turning her attention to Alex as he stepped through the door.

His clothes alone marked him as a man of distinction. As did a reputation for being generous, which preceded him into any establishment in Royal. Had they a red carpet in the back room, Stephanie suspected the fawning clerk would have been on her hands and knees rolling it out before Alex's every step. The only thing keeping her from acting on the snooty clerk's suggestion to leave posthaste was her husband-to-be's gaze pinning her like a butterfly inside a cigar box for a science-fair project.

''Tell me that I didn't actually hear you suggest that my fiancée take her business elsewhere.''

Disdain dripped from Alex's cultured voice in poisonous beads.

''Of c-course not, Mr. Kent,'' the woman stammered.

Bewildered, she waited for the lucky lady to appear behind him. Her lips curved into a thin, welcoming smile.

Stepping around the clerk to claim this wayward fashion pariah as his own, Alex abandoned the woman altogether. He took Stephanie by the elbow.

The sallow-faced woman's decision to write her off at first glance left him seething. Familiar with all aspects of snobbery, Alexander was bothered that his wife-to-be considered herself unworthy of the clerk's courtesy.

"Follow me," he demanded, steering her toward the front of the store.

Grateful, Stephanie made for the door. Even on sale, the few garments she had priced cost more than her three summer paychecks combined. Nothing would give her more pleasure than to leave the gaping salesclerk alone in the shop to lament an enormous lost commission.

"Stand still," Alex said, directing Stephanie to the racks where the latest and most expensive fashions were displayed.

He studied her figure. That was no small task considering the oversize sweater she so effectively used to hide it. To his surprise, beneath all that excessive material was a lovely feminine shape.

"Bring her a size nine in that," he told the saleslady, gesturing to a mannequin dressed in a sumptuous dress of indigo silk.

Its flowing lines were classic in design. To Stephanie, it looked better suited to a runway model than a simple working woman. When she started to protest, Alexander placed a hand on the middle of her back and nudged her gently but firmly toward the changing room.

"Now, honey bear," he crooned. "You just let me pick out a few things for your trousseau without worrying your pretty little head about what it costs."

Stephanie groaned inwardly. His chauvinistic attitude wasn't the only thing rankling her. As much as she wanted to remind Alex that she was not the typical fashion plate he was used to dating, she could think of no way to politely point that out to her fiancé without raising both of the salesclerk's plucked eyebrows. So rather than make a fuss, she accepted the silk garment with a bright smile.

Alexander noted how Stephanie carefully draped the silken garment over her arm as if fearing she might crease it. The way she let her gaze linger upon it with undisguised longing stirred something inside him. Having witnessed other women toss upon the floor the designer clothes he bought for them as if the garments were nothing more than rags, Alexander found Stephanie's precautions endearing. He was struck by the fact that she didn't seem particularly thrilled at the prospect of spending someone else's money on herself. Such frugality in light of the unlimited budget at her disposal made Alexander all the more determined to buy this woman whatever her heart desired.

"Now, don't be shy," he called through the flimsy curtains of the changing room. "Hurry on out and let me have a look at you, sweetheart."

The endearment felt as slick as the fabric Stephanie held in her hands—and as soft to the touch. As realistic as she was about her feminine shortcomings, the woman in her couldn't help responding to the sweet nothings that rolled off his tongue. How many times in her daydreams had she imagined a man calling out to her in just such a tender tone? She didn't suppose someone as worldly as Alexander Kent could possibly understand how his attempt at credible play-acting might trigger aspirations of such a modest nature. Stephanie had no doubt that he would scoff at them if she dared put them into words. Not one to ask for the moon and the stars, she longed only for a good man to love her for who she was—not what he could shape her into becoming.

Alexander's insistence that she model for him left little wiggle room to pretend that she had tried on the dress and found it somehow lacking.

"Do you need help with the zipper?"

Alex's voice conjured up images of his hands resting upon the small of her back, searching for the device the seamstress had so expertly hidden in a fold of bright satin and locating instead the clasp to her bra. A vision of one of his hands slipping beneath the opening of the frock to caress her breasts had Stephanie breathing rapidly. In her mind's eye, she could see him standing behind her in the mirror, nuzzling her neck and whispering some suggestive proposition as clearly as she could see her own reflection.

"If so, I'd be glad to help."

Startled out of her erotic daydream by that offer, Stephanie slipped the dress over her head and employed the voice she used when a child misbehaved in the library. "Don't even think about it, mister."

A moment later she emerged from behind the curtain as if she were stepping in front of a firing squad. Still, she couldn't help noticing with pleasure the way Alexander's eyes widened in appreciation as she finished cinching her belt.

"Very nice."

Alex was not referring to the dress at all. His gaze lingered upon the way the garment hugged her curves possessively. Why so many of the women he dated were obsessed with looking like sticks was beyond him. The female shape was never designed to be angular and bony. He was amazed that Stephanie went to such lengths to cover up her voluptuous body with such baggy, understated clothes.

"How about a pair of shoes to match?" he suggested.

The clerk scuttled off to do his bidding without so much as asking Stephanie what size she wore. She returned in a moment clutching an assortment of boxes to her chest. The woman's deference to Alexander was, in its own way, as irritating as her earlier hostility to Stephanie. Having little to say in the matter, Stephanie suddenly found herself caught in a cyclone of clothing. Colors swirled about her as Alexander pitched designer fashions at her faster than she could try them on.

"This is way too much," she said each time she materialized from behind the curtain to secure his opinion.

"And those are way too little," she gasped, spying the sexy undergarments he was directing the saleslady to include with his purchases.

Apparently not satisfied with buying her a paltry week's clothing for their mission, Alexander seemed intent upon replacing Stephanie's entire wardrobe with a year's supply of the most sumptuous fashions she had ever seen. When the pile of clothes upon the sales counter grew so high it looked as if it might topple over, the clerk began another. And another. And another.

Alarmed by the excess, Stephanie waited until the saleslady went off on yet another of Alexander's errands before pointing out the obvious to her overly generous benefactor.

"This is beautiful," she said, gesturing to an elegant outfit. "But pray tell where will I ever wear it once our mission is over?"

Alexander looked at her as if he couldn't believe she had broached the subject. Never before had a woman questioned his largesse.

"To school," he told her. "Or the country club or a bake sale, for all I care. As my wife it is important that you look the part."

To that end he pulled out a cell phone and booked an "emergency" appointment with the most sought-after hairstylist in town. Satisfied that the role of Pygmalion suited him well, he turned to her with an expectant smile. He was surprised that Stephanie did not return his smile.

The fact that he had her prancing around in front of him in such exquisite styles left her feeling like one of her Barbie dolls. As a child she used to spend hours dressing them up and marching them through impossible happy-ever-laughter plots derived from what her mother coined an "overactive" imagination. If only her staid, protective mother could see her now! Even in her wildest flights of childhood fancy, Stephanie could not have envisioned such a scenario.

They left the shop a short while later with a stag-

gering number of bags and boxes filling the trunk of
Alex's black Jaguar. Several found a temporary home
upon the leather back seat. Before Stephanie could
see the sales receipt, Alex had deposited it in a trash
can and settled her into the passenger seat of his
sports car.

In the privacy of the vehicle, she took a deep breath
and voiced her growing concern.

"Costuming is one thing, but I draw the line at
letting anyone mess with my hair, Alex."

Long and straight and luxurious, it was Stephanie's
secret vanity. Though she often pulled it back into a
ponytail or a bun for work, she loved the way it felt
at night when she combed it out and let it fall down
around her shoulders, transforming her from a sensi-
ble being to a sensual one.

Alexander refused to listen to her qualms, maintaining that any other woman would be ecstatic at the
opportunity to have Mr. Karol give them a personal
makeover. It was very likely that the popular hairstylist had risked the ire of some wealthy matriarch
in making room for Stephanie at Alex's request.

"You of all people should know just how important this is in setting the proper effect. You wouldn't
let Juliet come out onstage wearing some ultrachic
bob any more than I would allow you to enter into
this marriage looking anything less than fabulous."

While Alexander's taste in clothing might be im-
peccable, a vision of herself sporting an extreme runway haircut flashed though Stephanie's mind. She
might not be a beauty queen, but was nevertheless

hurt by the fact that this man didn't appreciate what she considered to be her best feature.

"What's wrong with my hair?" she demanded to know.

"Absolutely nothing."

Leaning across the front seat, Alex freed a strand tucked behind her ear. It felt as soft as one of the silk dresses that he had just purchased for her. The color of perfectly aged whiskey, it matched her brown eyes in hue and mellowness. Fascinated how Stephanie's hair caught the sunshine streaming in through the windows and held both the light and his attention captive, Alex felt a shiver run through him. His eyes met hers. The vulnerability in their depths coaxed a purely masculine reaction from him over which he had no control.

Clearing his throat, he attempted to assume the dispassionate air of a seasoned FBI agent preparing for duty.

"Absolutely nothing that anyone except the very wealthy could discern. The last thing I want to do is hurt your feelings, but the difference between a good cut and what a first-rate stylist like Mr. Karol can do with such beautiful hair as yours is the difference between the clothes we just bought and the ones you wore into the boutique that I asked the salesclerk to dispose of for you."

"You had no right! Those clothes were perfectly serviceable," she protested, cheeks flushing.

Stephanie's anger at his throwing away her possessions was nothing compared to her fury at the heavy-handed way he was trying to make her over in the image of something she could never be—one of his former girlfriends.

"*Serviceable* is the operative word," Alex retorted, running a hand through his thick hair again. "Look, if we can't even agree on something as simple as this, how do you think we're going to manage convincing anyone that we love each other and deserve the chance to raise a child? Why is it so hard for you to let me treat you to something special? Can't you just trust me that things like this really do make a tremendous difference in certain social circles? We don't want to give the crooks we're after any reason to doubt the authenticity of our marriage—and our ability to pay any exorbitant price they set for a stolen baby."

In the breath of Alexander's tirade, Stephanie went from feeling attractive to awkward and out of place in her new cashmere sweater and soft suede slacks.

"My father always said that only a fool would try to make a thoroughbred racer out of an old plow horse, but if you're intent on trying, far be it from me to try and stop you."

"That's hardly the issue," Alex protested.

It pained him to see the sparkle in Stephanie's eyes snuffed out. He hated being the one responsible for extinguishing it and seeing it replaced with such naked pain. Unused to feeling like a cad for simply offering to help a lady look her best, Alexander was at a loss. His attempt at making pleasant small talk as he drove to Mr. Karol's Beauty Boutique salon was miserable. He suspected the reason that Stephanie turned her head to gaze out the window was to avoid letting him see her tears. A man known for his charm, he suddenly felt all thumbs when it came to handling this enigmatic librarian/drama coach/changeling.

Silence filled the space between them. It was as vast as Stephanie imagined the gulf separating their social spheres. A new wardrobe and haircut weren't going to breach that distance any more than trading in her old glasses for contact lenses had changed her into Cinderella overnight. A few short blocks later, she allowed herself to be led into the inner sanctum of Mr. Karol's salon. She did so with all the enthusiasm of a lamb being led to the slaughter.

Doing his best to maintain the image of a doting fiancé, Alex called after her, "Have fun, sweetheart."

Grateful to have a little time to himself, Alex watched her go and then headed to the Texas Cattleman's Club for a stiff drink and the information he would need in Vegas if they were going to track down the criminals who had stolen Natalie's baby. That was, if they could actually manage to book an appointment while they were in the area. *If* they could actually convince anyone he and Stephanie were more suited for one another than vinegar and oil. *If* he could convince his partner to lighten up a little and have some fun with this portion of their mission before it turned dangerous.

If...

Alexander thought it odd that such a small word should carry so much weight. The thought of putting Stephanie near more peril than Mr. Karol's scissors made his stomach do an unexpected turn. He couldn't help but worry that for all her bravado, this particular lady would be utterly defenseless in a world inhabited by criminals not confined between the pages of one of the books shelved in the library. This fierce sense of protectiveness was the reason Alex had felt compelled to join the ranks of the Cattlemen in the first place.

"Anything special you want for your bachelor party, you just let me know," kidded Ryan Evans.

Clint Andover, CEO of a large security company, couldn't resist chiming in. "Wonder how many ways crow can be served?" he asked, referring to his old friend's claim he would never marry. Ever since Clint had remarried, his associates at the Texas Cattleman's Club had seen a lighter side of him.

Ryan grinned, a wicked light in his eyes. "I hear librarians do it between the covers."

One beer and innumerable jabs later by his friends concerning his state of impending matrimony, Alex had safely tucked in his pocket a list that Natalie had provided. Each pair of names on it represented a child who died at birth and another child who was adopted within a very short time. According to her research, these babies were one and the same. It was damn little to go on, but Alex had solved cases with less in the past. By the time he left the venerable site of the Texas Cattleman's Club, he was feeling renewed conviction about the part he was to play in the group's latest quest.

And a renewed sense of duty to the sweet thing that had so bravely volunteered to work with him regardless of her own well-being. Only this afternoon he had heard the news that the real Doctor Belden had been found dead, murder suspected. Alex had every reason to believe the apparent homicide was related to the adoption ring the Club was trying to infiltrate. Although the man impersonating Belden, Dr. Roman Birkenfeld himself, was in the hands of the authorities, there were others out there that needed to be caught.

The beautiful creature waiting for him in the lobby of the upscale salon upon his return was almost unrecognizable. She hardly resembled the woman who had scowled at him the whole night of the school fund-raiser for which he had found himself volunteered by his fellow Cattlemen. Had Alex not bought the clothes Stephanie was wearing or put her in Mr. Karol's capable hands himself, he might not have believed his own eyes. The transformation was astonishing. The thirty-one-year-old woman trapped in the guise and mind-set of a middle-aged spinster emerged from her cocoon an exquisite butterfly, trembling with the anticipation of spreading her newfound wings.

Much to Stephanie's relief, Mr. Karol had not advanced upon her with an array of scissors and a tub of styling gel. Instead, he trimmed a couple of inches off the ends, gave her a soft body perm and shaped wisps around her face in a timeless style that emphasized her best features. Alexander had been right. Though not a drastic change in length, the difference between her old hairstyle and new one was amazing. When Mr. Karol turned Stephanie around in the chair to look at herself in the mirror, she'd hardly recognized herself. The woman looking back at her could have graced the pages of a fashion magazine.

She was secretly delighted at Alexander's reaction when he saw her. He did everything but whistle at her appearance. As much as the feminist in her resented the need for any man's approval, the little girl in her felt like twirling around in glee.

Not wanting to give her true feelings away, she gave her husband-to-be a discriminating look.

"They tell me I clean up nice," she said dryly.

Four

"Isn't that Stephanie Firth?" asked one incredulous voice after another.

"It couldn't possibly be!"

Stephanie heard the whispers as she and Alex followed the maître d' to the best table in the best restaurant in town. Famous across state lines for its French cuisine, Claire's boasted an elegant atmosphere that was far different from the Royal Diner where Stephanie usually grabbed a bite to eat. A single long-stemmed rose positioned in the center of each spotless white-linen tablecloth surely matched the red spots on her cheeks. Feeling as self-conscious and out of place as Cinderella at her first ball, she tipped her chin up in defiance at the loose-jawed looks that tracked her to the chair that Alex pulled out for her in true gentleman fashion.

"How could you possibly confuse that drab-looking librarian with the gorgeous creature with Alexander Kent?"

"That *is* Alex, isn't it?"

"I heard he was available again. Who *is* that with him?"

Stephanie pretended not to hear the unkind remarks from a nearby table. Just as she pretended that they didn't hurt either. It seemed as good a time as any to convince Alex that she had the necessary performance skills to make her a worthy partner on this case.

She did not see the killing look he gave the two women seated next to them. Instantly their snide laughter subsided. Alex ordered a bottle of Claire's most expensive champagne and proceeded to engage in witty repartee that Stephanie assumed was intended to familiarize their audience with the idea that they were a couple. It was, in fact, intended to put her at ease. A glass of champagne did more to that end than any clever remark Alex could make.

Halfway through a scrumptious meal of pork medallions smothered in a rich sauce, sautéed asparagus tips, and wild mushrooms and rice, Stephanie felt better. Albeit an act put on for the benefit of the public, Alexander *was* naturally charming. His wry sense of humor helped her unwind, and she found little need to rely on her acting ability to feign a good time.

For his part, Alex was surprised by Stephanie's unexpected sense of humor. Her laughter was genuine and unaffected, and she truly seemed unaware of how lovely she looked. Alex found her transformation amazing. Not only had his partner's appearance undergone a dramatic change, her whole personality had improved with the makeover. She seemed far less defensive. And a whole lot more fun to be with.

It didn't take Alex long to discover that the way she looked at the world was entirely different from that of the women he usually took on such outings. Without necessarily meaning to, she challenged the way he saw life as well. And she made him laugh with a quick wit that kept him on his toes throughout the conversation. Surprisingly enough, his date was proving as intoxicating as the second glass of champagne she allowed herself to have. She was utterly enchanting. Alexander found her candor as refreshing as her take on life.

"I've always wondered what it would be like to dine in such a fancy place—with such a handsome man," she admitted.

Her eyes sparkled more in the candlelight than the glass of champagne he held. Considering that she was knowingly putting herself in danger, Alex found her sincere appreciation humbling.

As much as Alexander was enjoying himself, however, he never lost sight of the fact that they were the center of everybody else's attention. Glad that Stephanie had put aside her personal aversion to him, he couldn't decide whether she was really that fine an actress or if she truly was as intriguing a creature as he suspected. There was one surefire way to find out. His lips twitched with amusement as he reached into his breast pocket and drew out a small box covered in black velvet.

He presented it to Stephanie over a piece of white-chocolate cheesecake that she was openly savoring. He couldn't remember the last time he'd been with a woman secure enough in her own body to enjoy the taste of sugar without a plethora of guilt-ridden promises to diet the next day.

"What's this?" she asked.

She looked adorably confused.

"Open it," he suggested.

Everyone in the restaurant seemed to hold their breath as Stephanie reached across the table. Her hand shook as she took the proffered gift. She trembled, fumbling with the tiny pearl button that unlocked the delicate casing. Opening it at last, she gasped.

Not even in a magazine had Stephanie seen a bigger diamond. Or one more exquisite.

She was not the only one stunned by the extravagance of the present. Her gasp was echoed throughout the restaurant. Alexander could almost hear the printing presses firing up in the background. He smiled with the knowledge that the morning edition would be too late for most of its readership. Gossip in Royal easily outran brushfires devouring the open range. Cell phones materialized from stylish purses at every other table.

With their audience on the edge of their seats, Alexander cleared his throat and slipped from his chair to bend one knee upon the polished wooden floor.

Acting be damned, he felt ridiculously romantic as he took both of her hands in his own.

"Stephanie Firth," he said for the benefit of those unable to see her for who she really was. "Will you marry me?"

The expression on her face was priceless. Her eyes softened to the color and texture of melted chocolate, and her mouth formed a perfect kissable O. Unshed tears glistened in the candlelight.

Even cynics claiming to favor plainspoken reality over girlish fantasy secretly cherish hopes of just such a moment actually occurring in their dull, predictable lives. The line between acting and realism is a blurry one that many professional actors routinely cross. Newspapers are littered with accounts of leading men and women carrying passionate onstage performances into their personal lives. Wanting to believe in Hollywood happily-ever-afters, the public laps it up and begs for more. So it was that Stephanie was rendered speechless as she looked into Alexander's hypnotic eyes and imagined herself falling in love.

She slipped the ring onto her finger and was surprised to find that it fit perfectly. An enormous marquis spanning the distance between her knuckles, the two-and-a-half karat diamond sparkled so brilliantly that she wondered whether the reflection couldn't be seen from a distance high above the planet. Blinking, she forced herself to remember where she was—and why she was there. Telling herself that this fabulous ring was nothing more than a zirconium knockoff, she did her best to remember her part in this unscripted dramatic performance. The last thing she wanted to do was disappoint her leading man before the curtain fell on act 1.

"Of course I'll marry you," she said, shyly dropping her eyelashes so that Alex couldn't see just how caught up in the fantasy she had allowed herself to become.

"You've made me the happiest man alive," he replied so smoothly that the trite line sounded sincere even to ears that knew better.

Other ears strained to overhear the conversation. Reactions varied from widows who sighed and dabbed tearfully at the memories Alexander's proposal evoked. Younger women looked either shocked or cross. Their mothers politely mouthed empathetic expressions over napkins held to their lips.

"Let's make it look good," Alex whispered as he rose from his kneeling position to take her in his arms.

Stephanie panicked at the realization that he was going to kiss her. There was little she could do to prevent it. And little she would have done if she could have. If the truth were known, she had longed to kiss this man since the first time she laid eyes upon him in the kissing booth next to the poetry stand she and Carrie had run together.

"At least I don't have to pay for this one," she murmured so softly that Alexander could barely hear her, let alone any nosey parkers nearby.

Stephanie knew it was a lie.

She suspected that she would have to pay for this kiss for the rest of her life.

Alex didn't know what she was talking about. Nor did he care. The crowd they were playing to faded into nothingness as he bent his head toward hers. One hand slid down her back and pressed against her spine, shifting her closer to him. His other hand gently cupped the back of her head. Stephanie's long lashes fluttered shut, and her lips opened invitingly.

He intended to kiss her soundly and convincingly, but not with the kind of ravenous hunger that marked a man who had completely lost his senses in public. Drawing her even tighter against his body, Alex explored her mouth and found it surprisingly sweet— and addictive. Gentleness gave way to greed as Stephanie kissed him back with an intensity equal to his own. Her hands went around his neck, clinging to that strong column as if to a lifeline. Her body arched against his. A kittenish moan emanated from deep inside her throat.

Feeling her breasts swell against his chest, Alex was emboldened to deepen the kiss. Struggling for control, he stopped himself just in time. He tore his mouth from hers and gazed down into a face illuminated with passion. This woman was either the finest actress to walk the earth, or he was in big trouble.

A little old couple at a table across the way began the applause that registered in Stephanie's ears and echoed in her heart. That Alexander was looking at her with such a penetrating stare didn't do anything to calm her shattered nerves. A woman who had always prided herself on restraint and respectability, she couldn't believe that her body would betray her so completely. Had it not been for Alexander's self-control, she might well have found herself rolling into the caviar the waiter had brought to their table. Stephanie blushed at the thought.

Alexander's voice roughened as he whispered in her ear. "Shouldn't you take a bow or something?"

Stephanie looked as if he had taken his glass of water and thrown it in her face. She knew that a kiss had forever altered their relationship that had just recently moved from outright animosity to tenuous friendship. It also had shaken her belief that she would someday settle down with some unassuming, unexciting man. She doubted whether Alexander knew how he had ruined that humble dream by immersing her in a fantasy spun with gossamer and sprinkled with diamonds. She felt her throat knotting.

Knowing that tears would not play well to their audience, Stephanie did her best to restore the intimacy of a mere moment ago. "You didn't charge nearly enough," she whispered in his ear.

When Alexander responded with a perplexed look, she smiled. "Women would gladly have paid double for a kiss like that."

The bright smile she gave Alex seemed strained. It was all he could do to refrain from wiping it off her face with another kiss.

"Would they now?" he asked, his own lips quirking into a lopsided grin that made him look less like the playboy the media liked to portray him as and more like a little boy who'd discovered an unexpected present hidden beneath the Christmas tree.

The role of a doting fiancé was proving to be less of a stretch than Alex had first imagined. Although he knew that once their mission was over, Stephanie would never consider keeping the ring he purchased, he had made a point of picking out the most conspicuous stone in the jewelry store. Alex told himself it was only to fan the fury of gossip that was sure to surround their whirlwind romance and make their elopement to Vegas all the more believable. It actually had more to do with his wanting to see the expression on Stephanie's face when she was treated as a precious gem herself.

She hadn't disappointed him. In fact, her reaction had been so genuine and moving that it threatened to melt the heart of the most resolute bachelor in all of Texas. It almost made Alex wish that he cared and trusted someone enough to risk the rest of his life trying to make her happy. Almost.

The irony of his extravagant purchase did not escape him. Innumerable past relationships had come to a crashing halt the instant the woman with whom he was involved demanded a ring as a sign of his commitment. He imagined any number of them were going to be shocked and angry to read about his impending nuptials in the newspaper. It was all part of creating a credible background for them as newlyweds when they attempted to crack the illegal ring operating out of the adoption agency that Natalie suspected was a front.

As they took their leave from the restaurant, patrons stopped Stephanie and asked to see her ring. Pretending that it was too heavy to hold up, she propped one hand up with the other and proceeded to blind those bold enough to take a peep.

"How gorgeous!"

"Isn't she?" Alex responded, looking straight at Stephanie and causing her to turn a most becoming shade of pink. He did not see her blushing as a drawback to her theatrical reputation but rather as a charming sign of her inexperience with rogues such as himself.

Taking her by the elbow and maneuvering her toward the front door, he checked his watch and spoke loudly enough for several people to overhear the conversation.

"We'd better hurry, darling, if we're going to be on time."

"And just where do you think you're taking me now?" Stephanie asked, momentarily forgetting how quickly their plan needed to be put in action. Things were already moving so fast that her head was swimming.

"Why, to the chapel, of course."

Five

Not exactly the church Stephanie's mother had always envisioned for her only daughter's wedding, the chapel to which Alexander referred was in Las Vegas. He had a copy of a phony wedding certificate inside the bag tucked in the overhead compartment, eliminating the need for an actual ceremony. Even if it was just playacting, Stephanie was relieved to be spared the nightmare of a quickie marriage featuring a black-velvet painting of Elvis as a parting gift. Staring out the window of the plane, she watched her hometown shrink to the size of a miniature Christmas village and wished her worries could be so easily minimized.

It was hard to believe that only a couple of short nights ago, she stood on a high-school stage encouraging her hodgepodge cast of characters to continue working on their lines over spring break. She promised to be back for rehearsals in two weeks, at which time scripts would no longer be allowed onstage.

If only she had a script for what lay ahead of her!

As flattering as it may be that Carrie had volunteered her for this misadventure based on her acting ability, Stephanie quailed at the thought of sharing a hotel room as Mr. and Mrs. Alexander Kent. It was hard enough keeping this fantasy in perspective when they were merely sharing first-class accommodations on an afternoon flight. It was quite another when a honeymoon suite entered into the equation. Not that consummation of this make-believe marriage was even an option. Stephanie expected nothing more physical than a perfunctory kiss now and then in public to reinforce their cover and give credence to their claim that they wanted a baby.

The same kind of kiss that completely turned her world upside down and let think of little else since she had left Claire's dazed and dizzy.

Stephanie steadied her nerves with another sip of complimentary champagne. Two days ago she had asked herself what harm could come of an ugly duckling such as herself indulging in every woman's fantasy. Today she bleakly faced the answer to her own question. Flying first-class was just one of the luxuries one could easily grow accustomed to as Mrs. Alexander Kent. Not to mention the way people treated her like a princess in Alexander's presence. And how she suddenly felt as pretty on the outside as she always had on the inside.

It would not be easy returning to her lonely apartment and boring, predictable life once this mission was over. It was going to be impossible to forget the kind of kisses that were bound to render every other man's advances inept and inadequate for the rest of her life. Taking another sip of her champagne, Stephanie came to the realization that she didn't mind putting her life in danger nearly as much as she feared risking her heart.

She suspected that the only way of surviving with her pride intact was to convince Alex that she truly was the greatest actress in the world. Maybe if she could copy his cavalier playboy attitude and make it her own, she stood a chance of not looking like a complete fool. There was no reason a woman such as herself couldn't adopt that love-'em-and-leave-'em attitude such as his.

No reason other than the fact that beneath her professed cynicism that true love was nothing more than a playwright's invention to sell more theater tickets, Stephanie secretly believed that love was a sacred force over which foolish mortals had no more control than they had over the wind.

Her challenge then was to persuade Alexander that she was unaffected by him while somehow insulating her heart from the knowledge that she had already fallen under his spell. *Piece of cake,* she thought miserably, draining the last of the golden elixir from her glass.

Mistaking Stephanie's nervousness for fear of flying, Alex squeezed her hand reassuringly. The playfulness that marked the earlier part of the day had disappeared from her eyes. Those mysterious dark orbs were shiny with thoughts that took her far away from him.

"Don't you want to know where we'll be staying?" he asked, wanting to pull her back into the present moment.

Wanting to pull her into his arms and offer her a guarantee that everything was going to be all right...

The thought caught Alex off guard. Not the type to offer false assurances, he wondered why he felt so suddenly protective of a woman who insisted she was eminently capable of taking care of herself.

When she offered a noncommittal response to his question, he volunteered the information. "A brand-new hotel called the Lost Springs Casino."

"That's nice."

Alex knew very few women who didn't feel the need to fill their time together with conversation. Although the ensuing quiet was not particularly uncomfortable and did allow him the time to think through the details of initiating contact with the suspect adoption agency as soon as possible, he couldn't help but wonder where Stephanie's thoughts were taking her. They were certainly traveling in a different plane than the one which they physically occupied.

They reached Las Vegas without incident just after dark. Stephanie said she thought it boded well that their landing was smooth. Having never ridden in a limousine before, she delighted in inspecting all the latest gadgets in the one that took them from the airport to their accommodations.

Amused, Alex told her, "You're worse than a kid."

He couldn't remember the last time any of his dates had expressed such enthusiasm about the mode of transportation that got them to and from one social gala to another.

"I'll try to act more sophisticated when it's not just the two of us," she promised, fiddling with the stereo system.

Country music blared in Alex's ears, startling him and making Stephanie laugh. He accepted her apology in the same halfhearted tone in which it had been given. The casino where they were staying was the newest in the city and, as such, boasted every amenity even the most pampered superstar might demand. The closest Stephanie had ever gotten to gambling before was playing bingo in the church basement every Advent to raise money for needy children. The most she had ever won was fifty dollars, which she'd slipped into the donation box on her way out the door.

Stephanie craned her neck to see the sights outside the tinted windows of their limousine. Her eyes grew wide, reflecting the myriad lights beckoning gamblers to try their luck at each passing establishment.

"What's that?" Stephanie asked, pointing to a gathering crowd outside Treasure Island.

"Driver, pull over," Alex commanded.

A moment later they joined the ranks of seasoned tourists pushing and shoving to get the best view of the nightly show the casino provided free of charge in hopes of luring the bulk of the throng inside afterward. It featured a battle between two ships in the waters off the Caribbean. The young man who played the part of the pirate was extremely dashing. The

boom of cannons made Stephanie jump. She gasped
to see the young man's dramatic death scene when he
plunged into the water from an astonishing height as
his ship went down.

Although Alexander found the show cheesy, he
knew his companion was entranced. In fact, Stephanie
was so intent on being able to see that she didn't
protest when he wrapped his hands around her waist
and lifted her off the ground so she could get a better
view. Only after the show did she remember to grace
him with that enchanting blush that he was coming
to appreciate as a true indicator of her feelings. He
couldn't help but wonder if someone so limited in her
exposure to the world outside Royal, Texas, would be
able to disguise her lack of sophistication when the
time came to make their move among hardened criminals.

They proceeded to their hotel without any further
stops, though Alex made a mental note of all the
sights Stephanie wistfully mentioned that she'd love
to visit. To his amusement they included a roller-
coaster ride at the top of a casino at night, a magic
show featuring white tigers that were plastered on
billboards all over the city and a ride in a gondola in
the faux Venetian part of the Strip.

"Don't you want to gamble?" he asked.

All the women he knew enjoyed gambling with his
money, and he'd brought plenty along to fill the time
and add credibility to their cover. Besides he seldom
lost at the poker table.

"Maybe a little," Stephanie admitted, wondering
how far twenty dollars in nickels would last her.

The Lost Springs Casino, like other popular gambling spots, boasted a theme. Stepping into the lobby was a trip back to the turn of the century when the California gold rush made millionaires out of drifters, and enough gold dust sifted through the cracks of saloon floors to build one fabulous mansion after another along the re-created streets of San Francisco's posh Nob Hill.

Overwhelmed by all the lights and noises associated with such a high-dollar gambling operation, Stephanie mutely allowed Alexander to lead her to a front desk carved out of cherry wood. Behind it an antique gilt mirror ran its distance end to end. He checked them in as Mr. and Mrs. Alexander Kent at the hotel's finest honeymoon suite for the next two weeks without so much as batting an eyelash, and paid a bellboy to take care of their luggage. The desk clerk, decked out in authentic garb, offered the couple his congratulations and promised to send up a complimentary bottle of chilled champagne to celebrate their wedding day.

Stephanie blanched. If it wasn't already obvious that she was less worldly than the greenest ingenue, just wait till her husband found out just how modest she *really* was. Had she thought to bring along an old bathrobe that covered her from the neck to toes, she would have hidden every scrap of expensive exposing lingerie he'd bought beneath it. Since it was unlikely that the honeymoon suite boasted more than one bed, Stephanie assumed sleeping arrangements would be awkward, no matter how gallant Alexander might prove to be.

And having sampled his kisses earlier in the day, she had doubts about just how chivalrous he might prove to be under the circumstances.

He pressed a key into her hand and felt the tremor that ran through her. Then he smiled at her with such understanding that it made her want to burst into tears. She hated being so transparent.

"Would you like to spend a little time in the casino before heading up to our room?" Alex suggested.

Stephanie nodded her head gratefully.

"Let me get you some chips, and I'll be right back."

"Wait a minute," she said, putting a hand out to stop him. She dug in her purse and pulled out a fifty-dollar bill—more than twice what she had intended to spend. However, if that amount would prolong the time before the agony of accompanying him to bed until the wee hours of the morning, the extravagance would be worth it. With her luck, Stephanie figured the one-arm bandits would gobble up all her money in record time without a single payout.

Alexander refused to take the crumpled bill she held out to him. He gave her a crooked smile in return.

"I don't mean for you to spend your *own* money, sweetheart," he said, folding her hand back over the money before heading to the cashier's cage and leaving her to her own devices for a moment.

In the din of deafening background noise, the sound of his parting endearment was easy on the ears. Stephanie couldn't believe how incredibly sweet Alexander was acting. Although *acting* was the operative word, she wondered if it was possible that he wasn't really the rogue she had made him out to be in her own mind. Never before had a man treated her like a precious object, publicly cherishing her and indulging her every whim. Phony or not, it did wonders for a woman's self-esteem.

By the time Alex returned, someone had thrust a complimentary drink in Stephanie's hands and she was studying a slot machine trying to figure out how many nickels she should feed it to maximize her bet. It was all he could do to keep from laughing at the earnest expression on her face. It was all he could do to keep from taking her in his arms and hustling her off to their room where he could have her all to himself. The thought tightened his guts and made him feel as nervous as a pubescent boy on his first date.

Pressing a roll of hundred-dollar chips into her hands, he asked if she would like to accompany him to the tables. Unaware of how much money was at stake, Stephanie gave him a skeptical glance.

"Are you sure you know what you are doing?" she asked.

Alex responded on a teasing note. "So sure I'll make a wager with you that at the end of the night, I'll have more of my stash left than you do of yours."

Looking at the roll of chips in her hands, Stephanie figured since it was not her hard-earned money, the worst that could happen was that the awkward time in which they checked into their mutual room would be momentarily postponed. Truly, Stephanie had nothing to lose.

"What's the wager?" she asked, leveling a suspicious look at him.

Surprised by her willingness to take such a risk, he leveled his emerald eyes right back at her. They twinkled with mischief.

"If I win, you let me see you in one of those gorgeous nightgowns that I bought you." He held up a hand at her protest. "Mind you, I said nothing about touching—although that's an option if you'd like it to be. I'd just like to see you wearing something as beautiful and soft as my new bride herself."

Stephanie didn't know whether she should slap the man or melt beneath his compliment. Indeed, the wager was as tempting as it was terrifying.

Having packed nothing but the new clothes Alex had bought her, there was little risk on her part. Surely if they were to be spending the next two weeks sharing a hotel suite, the man was bound to see her in nightwear. Any reasonable woman would take the bet and consider herself the winner whatever the outcome.

"And if I win?" Stephanie pressed.

"Anything you want," was his unqualified reply.

Stephanie thought for a moment. Of all the things she could ask for, she thought it would be fun to choose something that would be nigh onto impossible for Alexander Kent to deliver. It was something that all women desire but lack the nerve to come right out and ask for it for fear of looking petty.

"If I win," she said, looking him directly in the eye, "I want you to take me to a dinner show of my choice."

This time she held up her hand to stop him from accepting before he heard the rest of her terms.

"And," she added, "no matter how gorgeous all the women onstage and in the audience are, you have to treat me like I'm the most beautiful one in the place."

Having expected something monetary in nature, Alex thought it the strangest request in the world.

"I can do that," he said, not missing a beat. "And I'll do my best to make you believe it, too."

He stooped to take her hand in his. Lifting it to his lips, he sealed the deal with a kiss. The tremble that ran through Stephanie shook through him as well.

Two hours later, Alex threw in his cards, disgusted by the most dismal luck he'd ever had. Fate seemed to be conspiring against him. He checked his watch before pocketing his handful of remaining chips. After an exhausting day, he expected Stephanie was as worn out as he was. It was time to call the bet, and let the chips fall where they may.

The thought of losing his ridiculous side wager left him disappointed that no amount of liquor could soothe. The truth was, Alex had made that bet with Stephanie simply to put her at ease about the necessary arrangements of cohabitating for the duration of their mission. He couldn't bear the thought of watching her dive beneath the covers every night in a desperate attempt to keep him from getting a glance at her in her nightgown. Someone of her sensibilities might go so far as to wrap a sheet around herself or drag out some awful bathrobe to maintain her chaste image.

Several of the nightgowns Alex had purchased earlier in the day seemed modest enough. Even if Stephanie chose the most risqué item she owned, he hoped she didn't imagine that he was going to lose all self-control and ravage her. Alex wasn't the type of man who forced himself on any woman, especially one as chaste as Royal's most dedicated librarian. One as clearly inexperienced and panicky about her own sexuality. One as utterly adorable in her excitement over the things that had long ago lost their luster for him. One as completely unaware of how beautiful she really was.

As Alex stood up to go, he heard the sound of a woman yelling across the noisy casino. It was an all-too-familiar voice.

Avoiding games requiring any semblance of skill, Stephanie had exchanged a portion of her chips for a plastic bucket of silver dollars. One hundred of them to be exact. Not wanting to spend any more than that amount over the course of the night, she'd vowed to pay Alexander back if she lost it all.

That wasn't going to be an issue. Alex watched Stephanie attempting to catch the overflow of coins spilling out of a slot machine. She was jumping up and down beneath a flashing rainbow of lights, bells were ringing, and the sound of a jackpot drew spectators from all directions, hoping some of that good luck would magically be transferred to them. The chorus of the song she was chanting went something like this: "Five thousand dollars! I just won five thousand dollars! Can you believe it? Five thousand dollars!''

As much as Alexander hated to lose at anything, it was worth the cost of his pride to see her in such high spirits. Her eyes sparkled even more brightly than the diamond flashing on her hand. That he had spent more than her winnings on her trousseau alone didn't seem to take away from Stephanie's conviction that she had just come into a small fortune. When Alex stepped up beside her to offer his congratulations, she threw her arms around him and restated the obvious.

''I won!''

''I see that,'' he said wryly. ''I guess that means I won't be seeing you in your pj's anytime soon.''

Wrapped in her arms, her laughter, and that haunting, subtle fragrance she favored, the penalty for losing that particular bet seemed truly lamentable. Had she not looked like someone who had just single-handedly bagged Santa Claus himself, Alex might have taken his defeat even harder. As it was, the prospect of having to pay up didn't seem much of a challenge. He suspected that Stephanie would be as awed by whatever show they went to see as she was by every other aspect of Vegas. As jaded as he was, Alex couldn't help but be charmed.

For all Stephanie's jubilation, one would think she had just won five million dollars instead of five thousand. The effect of that paltry amount made Alex recall how good it had felt to close his first big deal on his own—without any help from a father who saw no need for his son to work for a living. Stephanie wasn't as immune to the allure of money as she'd led him to believe. And it pleased him to see her so overjoyed at winning some pocket change.

"Today must be your lucky day," he told her. "Wish I could say the same, but I'm afraid Lady Luck has been stingy with me."

Alex hadn't thought her dazzling smile could get any bigger. He was wrong.

"Do you mean to say that I beat you tonight using only my seed money as the minimum ante while you were at that high-stakes poker game where I left you a little while ago?" Stephanie gloated.

Alex shook his head with regret. "You bested me fair and square," he admitted.

Stephanie threw her own head back and laughed, triggering a cascade of hair to fall in shimmering waves about her glowing face. Taken aback by the sight, Alexander wondered how it was possible that he ever considered this woman plain.

She gave him an enigmatic smile. "Don't you think it's about time we go to bed?" she asked.

The comment caused Alex's eyes to glow with feral anticipation.

"At last I've been dealt a winning hand," he murmured, holding out hope that if he were to play those cards right, they might both come out big winners before their wedding night was officially over.

Six

Alexander spread a blanket over the sleeping form of the angel curled on top of his bed and sighed. Stephanie had been so exhausted and giddy over her winnings that she had barely made it across the threshold before she was asleep. Pausing only long enough to kick off her expensive pumps, she mumbled, "I'm beat," over a most undignified yawn as she stumbled into bed without pausing to pull the covers back.

So much for any honeymoon fantasy the bride-groom had been entertaining.

Next to the bed a complimentary champagne bottle bobbed in a bucket of melted ice. For some reason it reminded Alexander of the *Titanic*. Absently, he peeled the expensive label off the bottle and considered drinking the wine alone. After all, what man doesn't deserve a toast on his wedding night? Especially one who wasn't going to get the chance to consummate his marriage?

When he'd first accepted this assignment, Alex hadn't expected to even like Stephanie, let alone be so attracted to her that he was fighting to control the lustful thoughts racing through his mind as he dutifully tucked her into bed. She was too tired to protest. He had never imagined what a good sport this prim librarian could be: surrendering herself to snobby salesclerks, pretentious beauticians and nosy gossips with such grace and good humor that it made him want to slay every dragon that stood in her way. Her obvious delight in the things that the well-to-do took for granted let him see the world with fresh eyes. It was virtually impossible to feel cynical around such a woman.

Her kisses left him sitting in the dark feeling more aroused and sexually frustrated than any other time he could remember. Stephanie Firth might just be the finest actress since Sarah Bernhardt to ever grace the stage, but she would never be able to convince him that her physical response to him was anything less than genuine.

Alex was a man who recognized honest emotion when he saw it.

And passion when he felt it.

Unfortunately, the instant he'd opened the door to their suite, Stephanie only had eyes for the king-size bed that dominated the room. Not that he could blame her. Even for an ex-FBI man, it had been an exhausting day—and he hadn't been the one who had been forced to endure a makeover from head to toe.

He studied her sleeping form in the reflection of lights making Las Vegas glitter outside their penthouse window. When he finally grew weary of torturing himself, Alex drew the curtain shut and considered his own sleeping arrangements. Along with a couple of chairs, there was a couch that looked about as inviting as a cold Texas bedroll beneath a winter's sky. That plush oversize bed and its sole occupant beckoned to him. Since Stephanie was still dressed and tucked beneath the covers, she surely wouldn't mind if he fell asleep beside her. Especially if he remained on top of the covers and left his pants on for good measure.

If not, she could always divorce him first thing in the morning.

Stephanie awoke groggy and disoriented in the city that never sleeps. A dull headache reminded her that she was unused to consuming so much champagne in one day. The sound of someone snoring softly beside her caused her eyes to fly open wide in dismay as she struggled to remember where she was. Who she was.

The clock on the bed stand read 11:15 a.m. in green, glowing numbers. A man's bare arm was draped across her chest. She peeked beneath the covers to check her state of dress and was immensely relieved to discover that she had all her clothes on. Satisfied that she had not been compromised, she considered the best way of extricating herself from such an embarrassing position.

She rolled over to face Alexander, intent on gently rousing him from his sleep. The movement didn't put so much as a dent in his deep, regular breathing pattern. She struggled to remove his hand from its intimate position where it rested on the swell of her breast. Feeling like mush inside, she was glad that Alexander was a heavy sleeper. She didn't want her involuntary physical response to give away the deep longing she felt. With his eyelids closed, Stephanie felt safe studying his features up close. Even in his sleep, the man was devilishly handsome.

Stephanie brushed a lock of his dark mahogany hair away from his forehead. It felt soft to the touch. She put the pad of her forefinger to his chin and tested the texture of the stubble growing there. As a little girl, she remembered the feel of her daddy's whiskers against her cheek when he came home late from working a double shift down at the local lumber mill. He would sweep her up in his big arms and swing her up in the air so high that she could touch the ceiling. Nothing had been more reassuring than his bear hugs and those long ago whisker rubs.

Years had passed since the day of his funeral, and still Stephanie lamented the feeling that she had been robbed of a proper goodbye.

In the far recesses of her mind, she could hear her mother demanding that she remove herself from this stranger's bed immediately. For once, Stephanie ignored the strident internal voice that had directed so much of the behavior that led others to find her aloof and reserved. For all the maternal and well-intended warnings about how men wanted nothing more from her respectable little girl than sex, her mother herself had enjoyed the intimacy of loving a man, if only for a few short years.

The warmth of this man's body curled around hers gave Stephanie a taste of what it would be to wake up every day in such a glorious manner. She didn't desire all the extraneous things that this pretend marriage offered. Chauffeurs and limousines and first-class accommodations and designer clothes were all well and good, but it was the closeness of loving another human with one's whole heart that Stephanie missed the most in her solitary life.

She damned Alexander for unwittingly awakening in her the longing for a husband and family.

Last year when she turned thirty, she decided it was time to bury that long-held dream. Having never experienced romance when youth and hope had been in her favor, it seemed futile to search for Mr. Right.

When she was younger, she had dared to dream a little girl's dream of finding Prince Charming and living happily ever after. How sad that adolescence had painfully convinced her to settle for less. Gradually, Stephanie had come to accept her lot in life. That of a prim-and-proper librarian with a dramatic flair and desire to help adolescents find their dreams before it was too late to make them a reality. The sad truth of the matter was that no handsome prince was going to come riding into her life asking for her hand in marriage. No more than exchanging the glasses she wore back in high school for a pair of contacts had transformed her into Miss America.

While Alexander Kent might not be her prince,

there was no denying that he was handsome and as wealthy as royalty. Stephanie held up her hand to examine the stunning diamond on her finger. It had to be a zirconium, didn't it? No man in his right mind would buy a rock like that when he was only playing a role that he disliked in the first place. It was only pretend. It had to be.

Why wearing that ring made her go all soft and liquid inside every time she looked at it was as startling as why her hands itched to touch Alexander's gorgeous body as he slept blissfully ignorant of her growing desire. She ran her hands across the smooth expanse of shoulders strong enough to take on a mob if necessary to protect innocent children and their mothers from being exploited.

Such selflessness cast him in the light of an unlikely hero.

The dusting of dark hair on his chest matching that on his arms was just as appealing. Stephanie's breathing grew shallow as she studied his mouth and imagined what it would feel like to have that mouth on hers. No wonder women lined up for miles around for a chance to taste those tempting lips. In sleep they lost the hard edge they sometimes held when he grew impatient.

Stephanie could not refrain from leaning in to press her lips against his. Eyelids that moments earlier could not have been pried open fluttered in surprise. Stephanie pulled away hoping that in his sleep-induced state he'd might think only that he dreamed such indiscretion on her part.

"Good morning, sleepyhead," she whispered. "Or should I say good afternoon?"

Thinking he should be allowed the same readjustment period that she required when waking up and finding herself intertwined in his arms, she did not fight it when Alexander's hold upon her tightened. There would be time enough to face the cold world in which criminals stole babies for a profit. Right now, all Stephanie wanted to do was indulge in the warmth of her make-believe husband's loving arms.

It had been a terrible mistake, if not simply a dangerous breach of etiquette, for Alex to sleep next to Stephanie. He berated himself for allowing it to happen. Hell, there could have been an old-fashioned courting board a foot thick separating him from her, and it wouldn't have lessened the intensity of his arousal one whit. He was hard enough to cut diamonds and frustrated enough to attempt it if it would possibly help get his hormones under control. All his life, women had thrown themselves at him, and he'd never been half as enamored with any of them as he was with the demure Ms. Firth who was at this moment staring into his eyes with the same look of concern that he imagined she would give any of her love-struck students when she mistook their symptoms for the flu.

None of the contempt he felt for himself seeped into the voice he used to address her.

"Good morning, my beautiful wife."

The dim light of day leaking through the floor-to-ceiling drapes allowed him a glimpse of the becoming blush to which he was becoming so attached.

"You don't have to pretend when we're not in public," Stephanie told him, rolling away and putting her feet where they belonged—firmly on the floor.

"I know."

It pained Alex to witness such withdrawal on her part. When most women made comments about how fat and ugly they were, he believed they were merely on fishing expeditions for compliments. It was just a way of extracting a contradiction to stroke an already oversize ego. When Stephanie turned aside his compliment, Alex suspected it was because she truly didn't believe it.

"Come here," he demanded, switching on the light next to the bed.

Stephanie reluctantly did as she was told. Alexander stood up and pulled her in front of a mirror strategically positioned over the bureau, providing the typical newlywed couple with an erotic view of the bed. He stood behind her and wrapped his arms around her as if fearing she might bolt at his next request.

"I want you to look at yourself."

Her eyes sought his in the mirror. Alex saw panic shining in their dark, sweet depths.

"I look a fright," she admitted.

Her hands went to smooth out the flattened cashmere sweater that she had so thoughtlessly fallen asleep wearing. Alexander had every right to be disappointed in the way she treated such an expensive gift.

"I'm sorry."

"For what?" Alexander's voice was tinged with exasperation. "For making me want to be the one who made you look so mussed and sexy the instant you wake up?

He refused to let her go until she recognized what he saw reflected in that mirror.

Stephanie wished she had a tissue to wipe away the telltale smudges of mascara that she had neglected to wash off the night before. Why Alex was being so nice to her when he didn't have to was beyond her. Such compliments merely propagated a fantasy that was bound to come crashing around her ears like some beautiful sand castle in the sky. It was enough to make her feel like bursting into tears. The sight of such a gorgeous man standing behind her wearing nothing but his rumpled trousers was a vision she hadn't imagined seeing anyplace but in her dreams.

"Would you mind if I take a shower before you do?" she asked.

Many responses to that particular question ran through Alex's mind. It was a challenge to force the only one that was socially polite through his clenched lips.

"By all means, go right ahead."

She slipped from his grasp like the proverbial bunny out of a magician's hat, leaving Alex feeling bereft. How many times had he awakened with some woman in his bed racking his brain for the best way to make such a nimble getaway himself? Was this the way they felt when he bolted on them?

Having the tables turned on him made Alexander

realize how his fear of intimacy prevented the kind of tender moment that he had just shared with a woman who seemed to be as afraid of commitment as he was. He amended that thought with a shake of his head. If the right man came along, he suspected that Stephanie would not hesitate to grab on with both hands and never let go. She was afraid of getting close to Alexander Kent, the notorious playboy. The thought made him immeasurably sad.

Not that he could blame someone so pure for wanting to avoid falling for someone the *Texas Tattler* delighted in portraying as a scallywag and rogue. While such an image suited his purposes as an undercover agent for the Cattleman's Club, it suddenly seemed awfully heavy to wear for the rest of his life.

The sound of water running in the next room shook Alex from his gloomy thoughts and put him in mind of more erotic ones. The thought of pinning Stephanie against a shower wall and having his way with her under the warm, inviting water was enough to make him groan aloud. Rather than tormenting himself further or satisfying his curiosity by sneaking a peek through the steamy glass at her voluptuous female body that he had cradled through the night, he reached for the phone to order room service. In a futile attempt to stave off a seemingly insatiable appetite, he could do little more than try substituting one hunger for another.

Seven

Stephanie stepped out of the shower a composed woman. There was nothing like washing away a good long cry in a cascade of hot water. Ever since Alexander had slipped that gorgeous engagement ring upon her finger, she'd given in to the temptation of taking her role as his wife seriously. She rationalized her behavior with a reminder that even the best actors and actresses occasionally succumbed to the pull of a strong character. Heavens, the newspapers were littered with articles about stars carrying their on-screen romances into real life. Their torrid affairs were the stuff of tabloids and television specials.

Her own fantasies were the stuff of an overactive imagination that she intended to get under control before anyone got hurt. Her own name appeared first and foremost on that list.

Stephanie tried not to be too hard on herself. A woman would have to be made of the same stone as the statues adorning nearby Caesar's Palace not to succumb to Alexander Kent's magnetism when he switched on the charm. Her heart twinged with longing that someday the part of the adored wife might become a reality, but it could not interfere with her reason for being here in the first place. Too many people were counting on her, to let her heart to get caught up in a two-week charade.

She was sure that someone as sophisticated and worldly as Alexander would scoff at her simple dream of settling down with a good, if not all that exciting, man who loved her for who she was. So Stephanie decided the only way to survive this ''marriage'' was to keep her heart safely out of things and never let Alexander pierce her emotional armor. By the time the hot water in the shower turned tepid, she was armed with a healthy attitude and renewed spirits.

Her newfound poise lasted right up until she looked around and discovered the clothes she had taken into the bathroom were nowhere to be found. Unsure of how to react to Alexander's little practical joke, she had little choice but to walk into the bedroom and confront him wearing nothing but a fluffy hotel towel.

''What did you do with my clothes?'' she demanded to know.

Alex almost spilled his coffee at the sight of his half-dressed warrior bride storming into the room. Wet dark tendrils spilled over white shoulders and framed fresh-faced beauty. Lordy, if his partner looked this good first thing in the morning without all the painstaking primping that other women insisted on before even considering the possibility of letting another human being gaze upon its imperfections, Alex didn't know how he was going to maintain the professional detachment this mission required of him.

"I had them sent to the cleaners," he said, hoping he needn't protect himself with a butter knife. He had never seen her looking quite so fierce—or lovely. "I ordered your breakfast, too. I hope neither gesture was too presumptuous."

Stephanie's mouth dropped open. It had never occurred to her that Alexander might simply be doing something nice for her.

"Of c-course not," she stammered. She sniffed the air appreciatively.

The smell of gourmet coffee enticed her to grab the bathrobe Alex had laid out on the bed for her and hustle back into the privacy of the bathroom. She returned a moment later. The white-linen cart that had been wheeled into the room was laden with fresh fruit and whipped cream and the biggest Belgian waffles she had ever seen.

Unable to resist such a tempting setting, she took a seat across from Alex and gazed out the window toward the skyline of the city.

"This is lovely," she said.

"Yes, it is," Alex replied, never once taking his eyes off of her.

That Stephanie appeared oblivious to his compliment didn't dampen her appetite any. It was a rare treat for Alex to eat with a woman like Stephanie. Once she got over the disappearance of her clothes, she settled into a delightful mood, pouring coffee for him whenever his cup ran low and taking every opportunity to rub in the fact that she had beaten him in the wager they had made last night. She had quite a time deciding upon which dinner show he was going to have to take her to as a result of losing that bet.

"What are you going to buy with your winnings? Maybe a fur coat or a special piece of jewelry to wear to the show tonight?" Alex asked, suggesting the first thing that came to mind.

"Heavens no!" Stephanie exclaimed. "I'm going to use that money to pay off the loan on my car. If there's any left over, I'd like to put it toward new costumes for our play. Juliet's skirt is on the verge of separating from the bodice in that old dress I've got her in."

She paused thoughtfully. "I do hope they are all working on their lines over the break."

Alex thought the way she had of biting her lower lip when worried was one of the most erotic things he'd ever seen. It made him want to bite it himself.

"I might be able to pitch in for such a good cause myself," he told her, hoping to entice her into splurging on a little luxury item for herself. "We wouldn't want fair Juliet spilling more than fake blood upon the stage of Royal's theater."

Stephanie laughed. "Indeed not!"

She was on the verge of telling him how centuries ago, kind benefactors had provided most of the costuming at Shakespeare's Globe in old England from their own wardrobes, discarding clothes they no longer wanted. Then she remembered her mother's admonitions that her interest in these kinds of subjects turned men off. Her mother was probably right. Alexander would likely appreciate a history lesson right now as much as she would enjoy a discussion on world finances.

Besides, it was time to discuss the business at hand. They were here posing as a married couple unable to have children. Their mission was to infiltrate the shady adoption service where their key informant, Natalie Perez, believed Dr. Roman Birkenfeld was selling stolen babies to desperate wealthy clients. Natalie could provide them only with the name of the agency and a list of names she had written down while she was in the doctor's employment. Now it was up to Stephanie and Alex to get hold of the hard evidence needed to prove those suspicions true and discover the rest of the culprits involved.

"Where do we begin?" Stephanie asked.

It was all she could do to refrain from using the corner of her napkin to wipe off a hint of marmalade from the corner of her partner's mouth. The thought of licking it off instead caused her hand to tremble as Alexander reached across the table and covered it with one of his own. Flinching at his touch, she recoiled as if a snake had just struck her.

A frown crossed his features.

"First I'll contact the private agency, set up an appointment, and try to convince them we're in the market for a baby. It would help considerably to that end if you could stop acting scared whenever I touch you. I'd rather they think we haven't conceived a child after innumerable and pleasurable sexual encounters, not because you find me some terrifying monster.''

Alex kept his expression bland, but Stephanie's reaction stung. It was disconcerting to think his advances could be construed as repugnant. A man would have to have ice in his veins not to feel something for the woman who had spent the night sleeping in his arms. A woman whose curves fit against the hard planes of his body as if she had been specially ordered just for him. A woman whose smile put all the lights of Vegas to shame.

Sleeping was, of course, the operative word.

Alex didn't know how much longer he could maintain control under such tempting circumstances, but a cold shower was in order. He stood up abruptly.

Stephanie apologized for putting that thunderous crease in his forehead. ''I'm sorry. It's just that I'm not used to...'' Her voice trailed off.

''Not used to what?'' he demanded to know. ''Having a man shower you with attention? Treat you like a desirable and—''

''Not used to a man period!''

That revelation left twin marks of shame burning on her cheeks.

It hit Alex between the eyes like a bullet with his name on it.

While he accepted without question that his partner was a woman of virtue, it had never occurred to him that she might still be a virgin. He would rather face the Mafia single-handedly than have to deal with the emotional impact of this complication. Mr. Use 'Em

The Silhouette Reader Service™—Here's How It Works:

Accepting your 2 free books and gift places you under no obligation to buy anything. You may keep the books and gift and return the shipping statement marked "cancel." If you do not cancel, about a month later we'll send you 6 additional books and bill you just $3.57 each in the U.S., or $4.24 each in Canada, plus 25¢ shipping & handling per book and applicable taxes if any.* That's the complete price and — compared to cover prices of $4.25 each in the U.S. and $4.99 each in Canada — it's quite a bargain! You may cancel at any time, but if you choose to continue, every month we'll send you 6 more books, which you may either purchase at the discount price or return to us and cancel your subscription.

*Terms and prices subject to change without notice. Sales tax applicable in N.Y. Canadian residents will be charged applicable provincial taxes and GST.

OFFICIAL OPINION POLL

ANSWER 3 QUESTIONS AND WE'LL SEND YOU
2 FREE BOOKS AND A FREE GIFT!

0074823 |||||■|||■||| |||■||||| |||■|||| FREE GIFT CLAIM # **3953**

YOUR OPINION COUNTS!

Please check TRUE or FALSE below to express your opinion about the following statements:

Q1 Do you believe in "true love"?

"TRUE LOVE HAPPENS ONLY ONCE IN A LIFETIME."
○ TRUE
○ FALSE

Q2 Do you think marriage has any value in today's world?

"YOU CAN BE TOTALLY COMMITTED TO SOMEONE WITHOUT BEING MARRIED."
○ TRUE
○ FALSE

Q3 What kind of books do you enjoy?

"A GREAT NOVEL MUST HAVE A HAPPY ENDING."
○ TRUE
○ FALSE

YES, I have scratched the area below.

Please send me the 2 **FREE BOOKS** and **FREE GIFT** for which I qualify. I understand I am under no obligation to purchase any books, as explained on the back of this card.

326 SDL DZ3Z   225 SDL DZ4G

(S-D-03/04)

| | |
| FIRST NAME | LAST NAME |

ADDRESS

| | |
| APT.# | CITY |

| | |
| STATE/PROV. | ZIP/POSTAL CODE |

www.eHarlequin.com

DETACH AND MAIL CARD TODAY!

and Lose 'Em Kent wasn't nearly as callous as he'd like others to believe. Hence, his association with the Texas Cattleman's Club in the first place.

It was time he admitted to himself, if not to Stephanie, that what he was feeling for her went a lot deeper than physical attraction alone. The little boy who had been abandoned by his mother had grown into a bachelor who had foresworn marriage altogether. In fact, he'd often delighted in referring to that sacred institution as the worm that conceals the hook. Any woman who remained a virgin past her twenties was definitely not into one-night stands—or two-week Vegas stands for that matter. Such a woman was looking for a long-term commitment, a family and kids, not a brief affair with a playboy.

Alex knew only that, unlike the women he was used to, a true lady would never stoop to using a man just to get what she wanted. Nor could he rationalize doing the same to her. Just as he couldn't afford to let a runaway case of hormones blow their mission, he could not risk blowing the cover he'd used for so many years to mask his longing for a true and lasting love. Whether anyone at that old rag, the *Texas Tattler,* believed it or not, beneath the devil-may-care playboy guise, Alexander Kent was a complex and sensitive man.

"All right, Miss Drama Coach," Alex grumbled. "If you'll kindly do your best to pretend you don't mind my touch, I'll do my best to pretend that I don't want to touch you every second that we're together."

With that, he stomped off to the shower, not bothering to even turn on the hot water at all.

* * *

Stephanie was flustered in the wake of his admission. It wasn't as if she had never encountered a man's touch before. There had been plenty of sweaty hand-holding in her youth, and she'd kissed her fair share of toads, too, because she didn't want to hurt their feelings or cause a scene at the time. But none of those men had been as dashing as Alexander Kent. She certainly hadn't responded to any of them with the kind of mind-boggling intensity a simple touch from Alexander evoked from her. If she flinched at his touch, it was not because she found him unappealing, as he seemed to believe. Quite the opposite. She drew away because his touch branded her with a mark of desire unlike anything she had ever felt before.

The knowledge that he really did find her attractive was headier than all the champagne she had consumed on her wedding day. And far more intoxicating than the cheap stuff they had been served at the Vegas chapel where their mock ceremony had been performed.

They had been in town less than twenty-four hours before discovering that there was no listing in the phone book for the name of the private agency that Natalie had given them, so it was fortunate that the unlisted number she also provided was still in operation. The person who answered the phone when Alex placed his first call sounded professional and polite.

"You came highly recommended by a friend," Alex purred into the receiver. "My wife and I are only going to be in the area for a short time and we were hoping to set up an appointment as soon as possible.''

Stephanie held her breath as he paused. When he spoke again, it was to assure the person on the other end of the line that ''money was no object'' and to reiterate that ''time truly was of the essence.''

A moment later Alex scribbled down an address and a time on the hotel stationery.

''Good. The day after tomorrow then. I appreciate you expediting this. It means a great deal to my wife—and to me.''

Stephanie hadn't said a single word herself, and yet she was shaking when Alex hung up the phone. This time when he reached out to calm her, she didn't draw away. Instead, she sought his reassurance by squeezing his hand hard. Her lovely fantasy was about to take a grave detour.

''What do you say we swing by this address and scope the place out?'' Alex asked.

Stephanie answered the question with a nod of her head. Seeing as it was the reason they were here in the first place, there could be no turning back now. While Alex was in the shower, she had put on a buttery-soft pair of rose-colored silk slacks and a silk blouse of champagne pink that accentuated her dark hair and eyes. As the weather was a temperate seventy degrees, she took nothing more with her on the way out the door than her purse and a light cardigan.

''And so the wild roller-coaster ride begins,'' she said with a brave smile as she pulled the door shut behind them.

She hadn't meant for Alex to take that statement

literally, but he distinctly remembered her saying that she wanted to ride the coaster that looked out over the city from the top of one of its tallest buildings. After driving by the illicit adoption agency, they parked down the street a little way and studied the clientele drawn to its services. To Stephanie's surprise, the establishment was not in some seedy part of town. The nondescript one-storey building was as boring as the sand-colored brick it was made of. The upscale-looking couples who approached its front door did so less with the look of criminal intent and more with desperation etched upon their faces. The whole sordid business made her feel like crying.

Feeling her empathy seep into his own pores, Alex turned their rented Mercedes away from the staid brick building and toward what he claimed was sure to be the ride of her life. Stephanie didn't bother to mention she'd been on that particular ride since the day he had exploded into her life like a tornado alighting on the set of the school play. This whole whirlwind adventure seemed like a dream, and keeping her feet on the ground was becoming more and more impossible with each passing minute. There was little use in telling Alexander that she hadn't meant for him to take her cursory comment about riding a roller coaster seriously.

She would have to watch what she said more carefully in the future. To her surprise, Alexander Kent was turning out to be an excellent listener, never forgetting even the slightest request she made.

No wonder women were drawn to him like bees around a honey pot.

An invisible fist closed around her heart and squeezed hard. She would do well to remember that she was but one of many in a long line of Alexander Kent's adoring fans. And if she wasn't careful, she would end up being just another one of his conquests.

"In case our marks check us out while we're in town, we need to keep up the facade," was his standard response to Stephanie's repeated protests that he needn't go to any extra trouble on her account.

Ten minutes later she was clinging to him for dear life. Stephanie had loved roller coasters since she was a kid. As an adult, it was the one time she could forget all her inhibitions and quite literally scream with abandon. It is impossible to maintain one's dignity on a roller coaster, and that was the allure of it for someone like Stephanie, who spent so much of her life upholding the image of a proper role model. She suspected her students would have been surprised to see her flying out over the edge of a building, twisting in great curlicues and risking life and limb for a couple of minutes of pure fun. The fact that she was hugging someone as gorgeous as Alexander the whole time didn't take anything away from the experience either.

He looked slightly green when the ride lurched to a halt.

"Let's go again," she begged.

Alex acquiesced with a moan. He loved the way Stephanie looked all disheveled and wild-eyed when their coaster car came to a stop again and they struggled to get their footing on terra firma. He couldn't remember the last time he had enjoyed himself so much. Years of dangerous missions fell from his shoulders. For a brief moment he felt like a kid again.

And he had Stephanie to thank for it. A real honeymoon on a cruise around the world couldn't be any more fun than their raucous frolicking in Tinsel Town. By the time they got back to their room to change into formal wear for the dinner show Stephanie had finally settled upon, he was ravenous. The concierge had their tickets ready as they came in from the tranquil Vegas weather looking windblown and red-cheeked from their wild ride with destiny.

For the evening festivities, Stephanie chose an off-the-shoulder midlength satin gown that matched the color of her hair. A lace shawl with delicate golden threading woven into the black lacing added an antique-chic look that was thoroughly modern. A vintage necklace, bracelet and set of earrings of bold red and amber stones showed her fair skin to its advantage. She wore her hair loosely pinned up, reminding Alex of a perfectly serene profile carved into a cameo. A strappy pair of black-velvet high heels provided him with a view of the shapeliest pair of legs he had ever seen. He supposed she normally went to great lengths to hide such gams to keep all the young boys' eyes upon their books and not upon the librarian's lovely legs.

He was practically drooling when she modeled the dress for him. "You've made it way too easy," he told her.

Stephanie's forehead wrinkled in confusion.

Alex explained with a smile. "For me to live up to my end of our bargain. Looking the way you do tonight, it's not going to be any challenge at all to have eyes only for you.''

Stephanie blushed in the way he had so come to look forward to.

''I was only joking about that,'' she assured him with a wave of her hand. ''Not only do I realize that you are not dead and thereby not immune to pretty women, we're not really married either. It was a stupid bet, and I release you from any obligation you ever felt you might have had toward it.''

He was dressed in a dark pinstripe suit with a maroon silk shirt and a solid tie of a deeper shade of red. Not a strand of his short dark hair was out of place. As always he exuded an air of unquestionable style. In a word, he was the most handsome man Stephanie had ever seen. She felt like a princess in his commanding presence.

That look of appreciation he gave her was worth all the pain that devilish pair of heels was about to inflict upon her feet over the course of the evening. Indeed, Cinderella's glass slippers couldn't have been any more uncomfortable. Stephanie sighed over her own foolishness. Knowing full well that, like that fairy-tale archetype, her own fantasy was destined to come crashing to an end soon enough, she vowed to make the most of it while it lasted.

Eight

For the remainder of the evening Alex had eyes for no one but his lovely companion. The stars on the stage had nothing on those in Stephanie's eyes as she took in the musical extravaganza. They had the best seats in the house, neither too far back to see well nor so close that they had to crane their necks.

Stephanie basked in the candlelight dinner preceding the musical production. After great hemming and hawing, she had finally settled upon the *Will Rogers Follies*. It had everything: great writing, wonderful sets, incredible dancing, an amazing rope-trick act done with fluorescent lighting, and lots and lots of beautiful women. And with the way Alexander watched her, she felt like one of those women sparkling like a jewel beneath the stage lights. For once in her life she truly felt sophisticated and sexy.

She had as many layers as the flaky phyllo dough used to make the honeyed baklava served as dessert. And she was just as sweet. Alex knew no other woman who would have been as good-natured about finding herself immersed in a mission fraught with danger. In close contact with the Cattleman's Club, he had heard the horrifying news that Dr. Birkenfeld had somehow managed to escape and was on the loose once more. Seeing no need to worry his partner, he decided to keep that news to himself.

It wasn't as if they were all alone on this mission. Before he'd ended the phone call, his good friend Darin ibn Shakir had assured him that he too would be hot on Birkenfeld's trail. As one of the top trackers in the country, the ex-military man wouldn't rest until his quarry was caught. The only concern Alex had was the sheikh's propensity for working alone.

"There's too much at stake here to indulge your lone-wolf philosophy," he'd told Darin. "I'm bringing the FBI in on this."

Darin hadn't been happy. He wasn't a man used to having his decisions questioned.

"We will speak on the matter again soon. It will take me some time to get my sources in order. Then the game of cat and mouse can begin in earnest," Darin had promised him.

Despite a sense of foreboding, Alex felt reassured. The noose was already tightening around the "good" doctor's neck.

Gazing at Stephanie, Alex was engulfed in a wave of protectiveness that washed over him and spat him out upon a lonely beach. The thought of anything bad happening to this woman was more than he could bear. He took a sip of his drink and considered the work that was to come.

Stephanie was too engrossed in the production to give any thought to the dark underbelly of the beast they were about to encounter. The only monsters inhibiting her gentle world were pimply-faced adolescents who failed to put their books back in proper order on the shelf or neglected to learn their lines and deliver them with proper ardor. He watched her face as she absorbed all the dazzle of this top-notch show. He hoped she wasn't comparing her efforts with students to the professionals onstage. After all, her young cast back in Royal comprised neophytes, and her own performance in the days to come would have far greater-reaching consequences than of any of the paid players onstage.

During one romantic number, she relaxed into the hollow of his arm of her own volition. Leaning her head against his shoulder, she sighed contentedly. Alex drew her close and breathed in the scent of hair as fragrant as perfumed rainwater. It was no longer necessary to pretend that he was enamored with her. For the first time in his life, Alexander Kent was smitten, and it was the most frightening thing that ever happened to him.

Stephanie was tired of fighting her feelings. The attraction she felt for Alex ever since the day he'd sauntered into that high-school gym and puckered up for charity had not lessened a whit in the short time they had been together. She had tried to find him shallow and callous. He was neither.

Maybe he was just pretending to be blind to all the gorgeous women surrounding them, in an effort to make good on the wager he had lost. Maybe he was doing it in the interest of advancing their cover. Maybe he was actually coming to care for her. Whatever the reason, it made Stephanie feel cherished as a woman for the first time in her life.

She had spent a lifetime protecting her chastity as if it were a treasure valued above all others. Now she knew that even if Alex simply discarded her upon a pile of broken hearts, Stephanie had made up her mind to have him. She was tired of being such a good girl all the time. Tired of living life from the sidelines. Tired of protecting a virtue that left her feeling dried up and undesirable.

The ring on her finger might be a fake. It could just be a prop in their elaborate deception. But it gave her the courage to do what she had to do. If she didn't at least try, she knew she would regret it for the rest of her life. After just a few short days spent in Alexander's company, Stephanie was no longer willing to live in fear.

What greater gift could she give a man who had everything than the gift of herself?

And so it was that she curled up in his arms in the midst of watching a wonderful production touting the value of common sense and the need to follow one's heart. She leaned in, and over the pounding of her own heartbeat, whispered something so seductive in his ear that Alex almost spilled his drink.

''What did you just say?'' he asked as if afraid to trust his own ears.

''You heard me,'' she said, taking his earlobe into her mouth and sucking on it gently. ''I just might be convinced to model some of that lingerie you got me after all.''

His sharp intake of breath made Stephanie's heart glad. At least he hadn't laughed at her proposition or rejected it outright. He pulled her against him so that it was impossible for her to ignore his state of arousal.

The searching look he gave her when the lights came on left no doubt in her mind that he was as committed to the idea of consummating their make-believe marriage as she was. The ride home from the show was short and tense. As they crossed the hotel lobby, Stephanie reached for Alex's hand. The way he looked at her would have convinced his harshest critic that he was a man in love.

Stephanie leaned against him in the elevator, and he silently cursed the other passengers who followed them inside. Alex couldn't remember ever being so all consumed with the thought of making love. Thinking her a virgin and committed to putting their mission above all else, he had worked at being a perfect gentleman in her presence. That Stephanie herself initiated his racing pulse with such an erotic offer had him breathing hard as he inserted the key to their room and opened the door to an exciting new world of possibilities.

He turned on a single soft light in the corner of the room. Taking her shawl from her and dropping it upon the floor, he ran his hands the length of her exposed shoulders. A delicious shiver trailed his path. Gently he set her on the edge of the bed and bent down upon the floor before her. Stephanie's eyes were wide and glistening with anticipation. Sensing her fear, Alex set about putting her at ease. Holding a shapely ankle in his hand, he slipped first one shoe and then the other from her feet.

Then he began the most sensuous massage Stephanie had ever imagined. His hands were magic. Rubbing the sole of her foot and teasing her toes with expert seduction, he smiled.

"This is just my way of checking to see if you have cold feet."

It would be nigh onto impossible to get his libido under control, but if the lady said she was having second thoughts, he was determined to exercise the utmost restraint by marching straight into the bathroom where he would simply lock himself in a cold shower for the rest of the night.

Stephanie was unable to find her voice to assure him that nothing about her was cold. Including her feet and her resolve. Afraid to tell him that he was bedding a thirty-one-year-old virgin, she simply nodded her head and decided to let nature take its course.

She wasn't particularly disappointed that she never got the chance to model a single item of the sexy lingerie. Alex discarded all of the aplomb one would expect of a world-renowned playboy as quickly as he did all of her clothes. Oh, he was gentle; that much is true. He was also so undeniably eager to unwrap the present she made of herself that it settled in her mind once and for all the question of whether he really found her attractive.

"Let me look at you," he said, hoping those words would free her breasts from arms that remained demurely crossed in front of them.

Still positioned on the edge of the bed, Stephanie took a deep breath and did as she was told. She arched her neck as gracefully as a swan, reached up to take the pins from her hair and shook it loose. Glorious waves cascaded over her shoulders and down her back in a dark, tempting waterfall.

Aching to explore the shadows created against her fair skin, Alex heard himself moan.

The sound put an enlightened smile upon Stephanie's lips, and she reached out to divest him of his clothes. Eagerly he assisted. A moment later his shirt and tie and pants lay in a heap at the foot of the bed. Alexander stepped out of them, a naked warrior. Rather than cowering in fear at the sight of him pausing to don protection, Stephanie silently thanked him for thinking beyond the moment and opened her arms to him.

Opened her heart to him.

And let him inside.

The feel of his skin against hers as he pushed her tenderly upon the bed and slid his body over hers was the touch of silk against silk. Before letting his hands go where they would of their own will, he ravaged her tenderly with his mouth. It was Stephanie's turn to moan. She caught the sound in her throat an instant before it turned into a sob. She hadn't imagined that the male body could be so incredibly beautiful. The poet in her urged her to linger over this moment and capture it forever with words, but the woman inside was too impatient and greedy to listen.

She set aside her worries about failing to please him and immersed herself in the pleasure of giving herself completely over to this man. To this tender, voracious lover who made her feel beautiful. Stephanie had read enough to know that her first time would involve a certain amount of pain.

The throbbing tempo of her pulse pushed her inhibitions aside. She gasped as Alex positioned himself between her legs. The size of his erection made her feel both powerful and vulnerable. Alex had proven himself a gentle man, but now Stephanie was impatient and arched her back in anticipation. Alex lowered his body to hers and murmured softly as he accepted the gift offered him. The sting and stain of blood were the sun rising on a dark, faraway horizon. Stephanie felt her body flood with light and warmth as she rose to meet him. To be so completely filled and so utterly aroused was something she had merely dreamed about.

Those dreams fell short of reality.

Alex never stopped kissing her until her own cries of ecstasy filled his ears and pushed him over the brink. Grabbing her by the waist, he reached for the pinnacle that she had ascended so quickly. He shuddered once and called out her name. A prayer upon his lips, it echoed the one reverberating in Stephanie's heart.

She loved him. Loved him. Loved him. Loved…

It was all she could do to refrain from saying the

words aloud. Fearing such an admission would send him racing back to the safety of a world in which sex played only a minor role between consenting adults, she wrapped her arms around him and matched the heart pressed against hers beat for beat.

No wonder Shakespeare's Juliet chose death over life without her Romeo. Once one's soul commingled with another's body in such a sacred act, there was no turning back the clock to a time of innocence. Sex in itself did not have the power to turn a girl into a woman.

But love did.

Alex brushed away the tears streaming down Stephanie's face with the palm of his hand. ''I didn't mean to hurt you,'' he began.

Stephanie laid a finger upon his lips to shush him. ''You didn't,'' she assured him.

At least not yet...

Refusing to cultivate such a sad premonition in the midst of a joy hitherto unbeknownst to her, she hastened to set his mind at ease. She didn't want him to regret this moment now or ever.

''They're tears of happiness,'' she explained.

Alex tried kissing them away. Despite her efforts to relieve his conscience, they tasted bitter and left the salt of guilt upon his lips.

''If you dare apologize to me, I'll cry in earnest,'' she told him.

Nothing was going to ruin this moment for Stephanie. After experiencing the most beautiful turning point in her life, she'd be damned if she was going to let him make her feel like some charity case. Come what may, she would never regret their time together. He had utterly ruined her modest fantasy of settling down with some inconspicuous man with a practical nature and a kind heart.

Stephanie would never be able to consider another man without comparing him to the one in her arms. She would no longer be content to accept any poor substitute for a husband. Nor to live life with less than an all out zeal usually reserved for players who strutted upon the stage and repeated the words written for them as opposed to those merely watching in the audience. No longer would she live life as if it were a dress rehearsal.

In the future, whenever Carrie's face lit up as she talked about her husband, Stephanie would be able to relate to her sense of infatuation. And when she and Alex made their way to that phony adoption agency in the span of one more golden day, she would not have to pretend that she wanted to have this man's children. Her fantasies were filled with images of an adoring family created by the love she felt for him. No acting would be required of her.

That Alex had cracked her heart wide open was a gift—and a curse that she would have to live with the rest of her life.

"Thank you," she murmured as she drifted off to sleep in his arms. Although Stephanie knew it was a most unladylike thing to say, that did not stop her from expressing the gratitude that enveloped her as surely as this man's strong arms.

Alex choked on the bile that rose in his throat. That such a gentle, beautiful creature was actually moved to thank him for stealing a gift most precious from her made him despise himself. After all, this was not a woman who used men like him for money or fame. This was not a woman who would ever abandon her duties as a wife and mother. Among the women who had frequented Alex's life from childhood until the present, Stephanie was a saint. And he a loathsome sinner who could offer nothing in exchange for the trust she had bestowed upon him but heartache.

It would not be easy for her to return to a lonely efficiency apartment and a library full of dusty volumes. Nor for him to resume a meaningless string of relationships with women far more interested in his money than in him.

When things had become too serious for his liking, Alex's last paramour had flung priceless objets d'art at his head and demanded some kind of monetary recompense for wasting her time on him. He suspected Stephanie wouldn't so much as ask for her heart back. The expression on her face when he had given her that outrageously expensive ring had been so touching that he could not imagine asking her for it back. When they eventually parted to resume life as they both knew it, he wanted her to keep it as a memento of their time together.

Such a grand gesture, he knew, was merely a way to assuage his guilt.

Alex lay awake long after Stephanie had fallen asleep beside him. As he studied her delicate features in repose, he struggled with the mess he had made of this mission. Never before had he violated his number-one rule of maintaining professional aloofness when working on a case. Adrift in blissful sleep, Stephanie did not hear the anguish in his voice as it rose in the darkness to ask, ''What have I done?''

Nine

Stephanie dressed with care for her appointment. She knew how important it was for them to look affluent, and while that wouldn't be a problem for Alexander, she knew that it would take more than clothes alone for her to pull this off. Prosperity, she was coming to realize, was more a way of thinking than simply spending money lavishly. Having been born into privileged circumstances, Alex understood this quite naturally. He carried himself with an air of confidence and gracious ease in his place in the universe that Stephanie herself had never felt.

Nor did Alex balk or haggle over the price of anything. He put quality before all else. Over and over again Stephanie visualized how she should act when outrageous sums of money came up in regard to the cost of ''buying'' an infant. It was crucial that she keep from showing any expression of horror that idea genuinely evoked. Just as it is almost impossible to convince a child that a potential kidnapper doesn't necessarily fit the profile of a stereotypical "bad" man, Stephanie herself struggled with the idea that the malevolence she was about to encounter would not be wearing a devil's mask.

Because she hoped to blend into the background and let Alex handle the intricacies of negotiating their illicit deal, she settled upon a beige skirt and matching cardigan that did more for her figure than she realized. Its classic lines and muted color made her feel a little more comfortable masquerading as Alexander Kent's well-to-do wife. The simple white shell that she wore beneath provided a place to hide the wire that Alex helped her attach.

"Try not to draw any attention to it," he warned, buttoning her sweater over the item in question.

Despite how small and unobtrusive the mike was, Stephanie couldn't have been more self-conscious had he pinned a conspicuous scarlet letter A to her. Nevertheless the husbandly gesture of helping her dress melted her. She gazed into his eyes.

It hurt her to see those green orbs fill up with guilt. When he averted his gaze, she reached up to grab his freshly shaven chin in both hands. She had come to love the smell of his signature aftershave. Like him, it was subtle and intriguing. Her dignity already in shatters, she saw no reason to avoid discussing the elephant that had crowded into the room with them.

"Please don't look away from me," she admonished. "I'm a big girl, and I knew what I was getting into. I've done nothing I'm ashamed of, and it's imperative to our mission, not to mention my pride, that you don't act ashamed of having made love to me. Personal feelings aside, we have a job to do, one that includes you pretending to be as crazy about me as I am about you.''

"I'm fond of you, too," Alex said, choosing his words as carefully as a soldier considering each step through a minefield.

Stephanie's laughter rocked him. It was usually this very moment in a relationship, the precise instant when he took one unmistakable emotional step backward, that he'd come to expect either fury or tears. Alex looked at Stephanie in confusion. Wasn't she going to grab the nearest vase and hurl it at his head? Never had he met a more unpredictable woman in his entire life.

Disconcerted, he refrained from asking, ''That's it?''

Clearly Stephanie wasn't going to fly apart like other women who threw their bodies at him in hopes of procuring a commitment. Alex admired the fact that she didn't overreact to his studied detachment. The lady had enough class and respected herself too much to sink to groveling or patent manipulation. Could she really want to be with him for reasons other than money and prestige?

The thought loosened his heart from the steel encasement he'd built around it, causing it to rattle uncomfortably around inside his chest.

Hand in hand an hour later, they walked up the sidewalk to the front door of the small agency that

Natalie Perez believed was connected with Dr. Birkenfeld's stolen-baby ring. Even though Alex knew Stephanie had initiated the hand-holding to create the proper appearance of a couple in love, he allowed himself to enjoy the rare wholesome feeling that the simple gesture evoked. It was a beautiful spring day, and he was holding hands with the most enchanting, perplexing creature he'd ever met. He doubted whether Stephanie had yet come to accept how very beautiful she was. She seemed oblivious to any man's approving glance in her direction—except his. And that made his own chest puff up like that of a young boy in love for the very first time.

As Alex held the door open for her, he prayed that he could keep her safe from the potential evil lurking behind it. The front office was adorned with the kind of chic furnishings designed to put wealthy clients at ease. A platinum-blond receptionist wearing lipstick a shade too bright gave Alex a predatory smile and looked right through the woman professing to be his wife. Stephanie wondered if the name pinned on her chest was anymore real than her bosom.

The woman took their names and asked them to take a seat in the waiting area. Her sharp eyes followed every step they took.

Settling into an expensive leather love seat only enhanced the picture they presented as a loving husband and wife. Alex put his arm around Stephanie and offered her one of the glossy magazines set out to distract them from a waiting period specifically designed to make them all the more susceptible to the sales pitch to come.

Refusing the proffered magazine, Stephanie instead laid her head upon Alex's shoulder. That her hand felt suddenly cold in his was the only indication of just how nervous she was. They both rose to their feet when an attractive, middle-aged man with distinguished gray hair stepped into the lobby and introduced himself.

"I'm Larry Sutter."

His handshake was as firm as the grip Alex maintained on Stephanie's shoulder for support.

A suit jacket covered Larry's spreading paunch. A heavy Black Hills gold ring flashed in the light as he bid them enter his office. Tastefully decorated, the room did not seem particularly overdone. Stephanie was surprised to see a family photograph displayed on his desk. She wondered if his wife and children knew he was a baby broker.

He waited until they sat down across from him to give them the bad news. "As your assigned caseworker, I have to be brutally honest with you. Although as a private agency our waiting time is substantially shorter than those of state-run institutions, you surely are aware that the availability of infants is in short supply everywhere."

Stephanie's face fell. It didn't take any great leap of acting ability to imagine what it would feel like to hear such a dire newscast when one's whole heart and soul was set on becoming a mother. Alex reached out to take her hand in his.

"My wife and I are desperate to start a family as soon as possible," he said.

Averting her eyes, Stephanie spoke softly. "We've gone to a good many doctors, and they all say the same thing. It's my fault that we can't have children of our own, and my husband is being so, so very sweet about—"

Her voice broke, preventing her from finishing the thought.

"It's nobody's fault," Alex corrected. "As you can see, Larry, this is an extremely difficult subject for my wife to discuss. I can't stand seeing her like this. Whatever it takes to speed this process up I can pay. If it makes things any easier for you, we don't care if it's a boy or a girl. I simply want you to do whatever it takes to put us at the top of your list for the next available infant. The couple who recommended this agency led us to believe that there was a possibility that we could return home with a baby."

The expression on Larry's face wasn't encouraging. "I don't know how I could possibly manage that."

"Get creative," Alex suggested in a tone of voice that left no doubt he was ready to do business. "As I said on the phone, money is no object. My wife's happiness is everything to me."

Stephanie didn't know how he could be any more blunt. Pulled into this drama on a visceral level, she could almost hear her own biological clock ticking. Images that she herself repressed on a daily basis because they were too painful to bear flooded her mind. She saw herself in a rocking chair, cuddling an infant and singing lullabies. A chubby fist clutched her finger. Eyes the color of Alexander's gazed up at her from behind long, dark lashes.

Lost in her thoughts, Stephanie imagined a sports decor for a boy and ballerina wallpaper for a girl. Children's books lined the shelves. Their two-story Victorian home would have a huge backyard, complete with a swing set, a fort and a trampoline. Laughter would echo throughout such a home. In each and every mental depiction, Alexander was at her side.

Time slipped by as silently as the tears rolling down her face.

When she'd first accepted this assignment, Stephanie's sympathies lay entirely with the women who lost their babies to such a monster as the one sitting across from her so coldly negotiating a deal. He reminded her of a snake all coiled up waiting to strike its next unsuspecting victim.

Sitting here, however, so immersed in her role as a potential mother-to-be, Stephanie felt a stab of empathy for any woman so desperate she would stoop to whatever means available to make her dreams a reality. Who was she to judge another when her own frustrated desire to someday have a family had the power to evoke tears on demand?

"Please don't cry, ma'am," Mr. Sutter entreated. "We'll get started processing your application right away. Once we get the paperwork in order, I promise I'll do everything in my power to try to make things happen as fast as humanly possible."

Shaken from her reverie, Stephanie watched the man slide some paperwork across the desk.

"Our normal fee is a hundred thousand dollars,"

he said, crossing that amount out and leaving it open. "But since you seem so anxious to speed the process up, additional fees would have to be added in later."

"I understand," Alex said indifferently.

So deep was Stephanie in her role that she blurted out an unthinkable question. "How much of this money will go to the young mother who gave her baby up?"

Alex could barely contain his scowl, but Mr. Sutter smiled at her benevolently.

"Almost all of it. Our agency isn't here to make a big profit. What we're really all about is making sure everyone comes out happy, including the mother who finds it in her best interest to give a baby up for adoption."

Alex wished the man hadn't said that. Not being as good an actor as Stephanie, it was all he could do to keep from reaching over the desk and choking the life out of that sleazebag. He'd been in the Royal Diner when Natalie Perez first came to Royal, clutching her baby in one arm and a diaper bag in the other. And ever since that day, he'd been unable to erase from his mind the fear and despair that he'd seen in her eyes. The only money Natalie received for the infant that someone had tried to steal from her was what she'd single-handedly made off with when she lit out of town with both her baby and the crook's ill-gotten gains.

By the looks of the paperwork Alex was in the process of filling out, they were mighty anxious to put some money back in the coffers, specifically in their own back pocket. The required paperwork resembled little more than a credit application guaranteeing the bogus company that a potential client had the money available to buy a baby on demand. Of course, this was one credit app that was never going to be checked out. All these sophisticated criminals wanted to know was where to send the paperwork to finalize the adoption after they had their money in hand. There was more than enough ready cash in the checking account that the Texas Cattleman's Club had set up in Alexander's and Stephanie's name to put any doubts at ease. These thieves obviously had no qualms about what they were doing and were more than willing and eager to accept the money Alex offered. He couldn't help but smile at the thought that it was the very money Natalie had taken from them that he was using to set up this sting operation.

"You understand, of course," Larry said, "that when the time comes, it will be cash upon delivery."

"Of course," Alex said, handing the pen to Stephanie and pointing out the blank where she was to sign her name.

"I'll be in touch with you just as soon we can complete our background check to make sure you are indeed a suitable couple."

When Alex bristled, Larry hastened to reassure him. "It's only a formality in your case, but we have to do everything by the letter. When it comes time for the actual adoption, you'll have to sign documents releasing the agency from any liability from that day forward."

"I'll sign them in my own blood if necessary," Stephanie said through a blur of tears that would have convinced the most hard-hearted criminal of her sincerity.

Alex gave her a searching look as he led her back to the safety of their vehicle. He hadn't realized how difficult this might be on a woman as sensitive and tenderhearted as Stephanie. He'd never been involved with a woman who expressed any desire for children. Most expressed the belief that childbirth was a surefire way to permanently ruin one's figure. None of the women he'd dated previously would have had a chance of pulling off the kind of believable performance Stephanie had given back in that suffocating office.

"Are you okay?" he asked.

"I will be."

She was shaking. Alex leaned across the seat to take her in his arms. Suddenly she was sobbing uncontrollably.

As a general rule, Alex was unmoved by the sight of a woman's tears. They had been used against him too often in what he'd come to think of as the big gun in the arsenal of feminine wiles. He had expected Stephanie to shed her fair share after making love to him as a means of manipulating him to his knees for a proper proposal to make a decent woman of her. He'd been wrong.

These tears shook him. These tears appeared real.

At a loss what to do, Alex simply held her tight.

"You were wonderful," he said, trying to get her to focus on the fact that their mission was moving forward as planned.

''I'm one hell of an actress,'' she sniffled into his shoulder.

Even though Alex suspected there was far more to Stephanie's performance than acting alone, he knew better than to prod. Personal feelings were not supposed to interfere with the job at hand. His never had before. That his own eyes were growing misty at the thought of making a baby with this woman was scarier than anything either Larry Sutter or Roman Birkenfeld could ever throw at him. Why that peculiar urge to father a child himself had grabbed hold of him right in the middle of their appointment with the devil himself was incomprehensible.

All Alex knew was that as soon as this mission was over, he would be free to resume life as he knew it, unencumbered by emotions that overwhelmed him and made him feel unsure of himself. Life without any obligation to anyone but himself and the Cattleman's Club sounded blissfully uncomplicated to a man unused to feeling a woman's tears pierce his heart.

Ten

Brushing up against wickedness, even when it was parading around in a nice suit and tie, left Stephanie feeling sick to her stomach.

"Would you mind eating dinner without me?" she asked Alex. "I'm afraid I've lost my appetite."

"Why don't I just call room service, and we can stay in for the evening," he suggested. "I have a feeling Larry will be contacting us very soon, and I'd just as soon be in our room as anyplace when the call comes in."

Stephanie wished she shared his sense of confidence. She didn't think her earlier performance would win any Academy Award, and she wasn't sure they portrayed a loving couple convincingly enough to lure Larry out of his hole and into the light of day. As lovely as room service sounded, all Stephanie really wanted was to be held in Alexander's arms until the sinister feeling that settled over her like a caul eventually went away. Embarrassed by her earlier display of tears, she tried rising to the occasion of their mission by putting on a composed face. The last thing Alexander needed in a partner was some needy creature clinging to him and begging for something he wasn't ready to give.

Stephanie thought she had understood the seriousness of this undertaking when she had reluctantly signed on. It wasn't until she sat in Larry Sutter's office actually "buying" a baby that the magnitude of what she was doing really sank into her consciousness. She supposed such haggling went on regularly all over the world: at local fish markets over the price of the day's catch, in clandestine chat rooms over the cost of weapons of mass destruction, and in sunny offices like the one she had just visited over the worth of a human being…

It made one appreciate the normal routines of life. She didn't know how Alexander managed to stay so sane and charming when his involvement with the Texas Cattleman's Club had him rubbing elbows with such unscrupulous characters all the time. She imagined it was part of the reason he refused to settle down with anyone. Beneath his polished playboy exterior was a man of greater character than she had ever imagined.

Stephanie assumed that he wouldn't want to entangle anyone else in such dangerous games. Who could blame such a man for not wanting a wife or starting a family? How would he possibly explain to his children that he had to leave them periodically to put his life on the line for a stranger in need? What wife wouldn't get suspicious and resentful when her husband refused to share the details of his secret missions for fear of putting her own life in danger?

It had never occurred to Stephanie before that Alexander might long for the security and love of family just as she did.

She wished she had a tenth of his courage. He had been right about her that day he'd accused her of focusing her energies upon a stage rather than living her own life. Up until now, she had found adventures only in the books that she cataloged or in the lives of her students. Stephanie wondered if any of them would recognize the spinster who had left them such a short while ago for the adventurous woman she had become.

Slipping back into obscurity wasn't going to be easy. Still, as much as she hated giving up her glass slippers, this Cinderella understood that when the clock struck midnight, there would be no golden chariot waiting to take her home. And while it made her sad to think that this wonderful, terrifying charade was nearing an end, she couldn't bring herself to regret falling in love with Alex—or keep herself from his bed. She would return to the monotonous details of her old life a changed woman, one who carried herself with the newfound knowledge that she was indeed beautiful. One who was willing to open herself to new experiences and risk taking. One who would never again let fear keep her from loving with all of her heart.

The instant they returned to their hotel suite, Stephanie reached out for Alex with greedy arms. She unbuttoned his shirt and tenderly kissed the flesh exposed by the subtle movements of her fingers. Alex's breath caught in his throat just as he grasped her hands in the act of undoing the button of his pants.

"Are you sure you want to do this?" he asked.

Eyes the color of Irish meadows held no hint of deception. Searching those piercing eyes, Stephanie understood exactly what his question implied.

Are you willing to accept me as I am? Are you willing to give me your body with the understanding that I will continue to withhold from you the deepest part of myself? Can you accept that our relationship ends the day we step back on that plane and return to our respective lives?

Stephanie nodded her head. She not only understood Alexander's terms, she accepted them as only a woman in love could. Glad that he had not spoken those harsh truths aloud, she gave the little girl inside of her permission to make the second of three fanciful wishes. The first had been fulfilled when she'd been transformed from an ugly duckling to an elegant swan. A newfound sense of loveliness she would carry back with her into her old life, surprising anyone who failed to look deep enough inside a person to discover their true beauty.

Her second wish was to know and be worthy of a good man's love. The questionable virtue of dying a virgin paled in comparison to having her heart cracked wide open. The act might render her forever incapable of living as she had before she had met

Alex—with a thin film firmly positioned between herself and the rest of the world. The old saying about it being far better to have loved and lost than never to have loved at all was the bittersweet refrain running through her head.

She didn't dare make her third wish for fear it would cause her to burst into tears. The likelihood of ever really becoming Mrs. Alexander Kent was too far-fetched to entertain even in fantasies.

Stephanie proceeded to unzip Alexander's pants, then drew them down along the length of his legs, all the while pondering their solid beauty. Kneeling at the altar of those sturdy tree trunks, she planted kisses upon both of his knees.

The beauty of the human body was etched into the details. Stephanie felt a surge of unadulterated lust wash over her. She longed to tease and to please this man as a lover would. A late-comer to the art of seduction, she was an eager study. Deftly she freed him of his briefs and placed another strategic kiss upon the swell of his desire.

"Stand up," Alex told her.

It was a command laced with tenderness.

Stephanie obeyed. Alex sat on the edge of the bed and returned the favor. First he divested her of the tiny mike placed so close to her heart that he imagined its wild beat was captured on tape along with Larry's carefully chosen words. He slipped her arms out of the jacket she wore and threw it aside. His arms encircled her waist. A moment later Stephanie heard the soft, erotic sound of a zipper's tug. Her skirt pooled around her feet, followed by her slip. Without bending down to loosen them, she stepped out of her shoes to stand before him in nothing but nylons and a thin white turtleneck shell.

"You are absolutely breathtaking," Alex said, making her believe it.

His shoes joined hers at the foot of the bed. Stephanie raised her arms to slide her top over her head. Her breasts spilled over a lacy demi-bra of traditional white. When she leaned over to kiss Alex's mouth, he hitched both thumbs on either side of her hips and dragged her silk stockings the length of her legs. She divested herself of her bra and panties while her lover removed the rest of his clothes.

Taking her in his arms, Alex pulled Stephanie onto the bed with him, not bothering to pull the covers back. He rolled on top of her, taking care to hold himself up on his elbows so as not to crush her. Her arms encircled his neck, drawing him as close to her as possible. Each breath he took in was ragged. Each exhalation against her skin was a gentle caress.

"Why can't I get enough of you?" he wanted to know. His jagged voice sliced through the lengthening shadows descending over the room.

Stephanie answered with a kiss, knowing the taste of the honeyed words upon his lips was the elixir that would have to keep her warm through the cold and lonely days ahead. Incapable of giving this man her body alone, she rated herself a poor actress indeed. Love poured from her fingertips and from eyes that beheld him in the light of adoration.

She knew better than to speak her feelings aloud. Such a move would surely be her undoing. So precious few days were left between them. There was no reason to ruin them by blurting out the absolute last words Alexander Kent wanted to hear. No reason other that the fact that her heart refused to be denied its voice.

"I love you," she murmured into the dim light and felt him flinch against the declaration.

Stephanie forced a chuckle intended to put his mind at ease.

"Don't worry," she whispered. "You're under no obligation to say anything in return. I know this can't last. Just let me pretend to be your wife in every way while we're together, and I won't hold it against you when we walk away friends when this is over."

In the silence that followed, Alexander held her so tightly that Stephanie found it difficult to breathe. He muttered something indiscernible, he appeared to lose some dark internal battle. Stephanie wasn't sure whether his invocation was a prayer or a curse. She didn't care. The only thing that mattered was being in the arms of the man she loved and becoming one with him.

When he drove inside her a moment later, she cried out, not in pain but in rapture. That she could push him over the edge of a steep precipice and ascend with him to a point in the sky beyond the mind's eye was magical. As he carried her to the heights of shared ecstasy, Stephanie cherished every detail of that wild, fantastical ride and pressed them in the memory book of her mind. Alex's eyelids fluttered shut and a startled moan escaped his lips as he exploded inside her.

Wiser by one day, Stephanie did not cry this time. Instead, she gave herself over to the delicious feeling of contracting around him. A woman could get no closer to a man than this: tasting the sweat of his body upon her lips, caressing the powerful muscles that willingly submitted to her will, revering the release of his body into hers, two bodies merging both physically and emotionally into one that soared high above the rocking earth below.

Floating back to earth, she felt herself a feather carried on an imperceptible breeze. Although she knew Alexander was thinking only of her welfare, she was sorry that he'd used protection. The thought of carrying his child made her glow inside. Oh, how she longed to take more than a broken heart alone from their time together!

The intense expression on Alex's face softened as he voiced his astonishment.

"How did you get so good so fast?" he asked, tenderly brushing a light brown lock of hair away from her face.

"I'm a quick study."

Stephanie smiled up at him, immensely pleased by the approval inherent in that question. With her limited experience, she was glad to know that she hadn't disappointed him. She kissed the tip of his nose. "Would you care to join me in the shower?"

"Get the water started and I'll be right there to wash your back for you."

So blown away was Alex by the intensity of their lovemaking that he couldn't force himself to move for quite some time. He lay on his back in bed contemplating the ceiling for a good long while, listening to the soothing flow of water start up in the next room. He could no more explain what was happening to him than he could expound on the virtues of poverty. The truth was, he was sorely disappointed in himself as a lover, something that had never happened to him in the past. Having solemnly promised himself to go slow the next time he made love to Stephanie and give her lingering pleasure, he couldn't understand how he had lost control of himself so completely in her arms.

When other women professed their love for him, Alex had no problem dismissing such claims as pure manipulation.

This time was decidedly different.

This time he was afraid that Stephanie meant what she said.

He felt like the lowest kind of heel. Playing games with urbane socialites didn't carry the responsibility as deflowering someone as genuinely sweet as Stephanie. Despite her protests to the contrary, he didn't expect her to march back into her old life unchanged by their time together. Once she discovered that men found her utterly irresistible, it was a given that she would quickly attract someone who would be able to give her a ring that actually stood for something real instead of a ruse. Having experienced little of jealousy in his life, it took Alex a moment to recognize the emotion that almost bent him double with its intensity.

Unable to get over the fear of hurting her and confused by her refusal to be angry at him for inflicting pain upon her without asking for a single thing from him in return, Alex sat up in bed and turned his thoughts toward the shower. As tempting as were thoughts of soaping up Stephanie's luscious curves, he doubted whether there was enough hot water in the hotel to wash away the guilt covering him like a layer of grime.

The ringing of the telephone interrupted his thoughts. Expecting a call from Larry Sutter, he answered it with a typical business tone. Dripping wet, Stephanie stepped into the room wearing only a towel. She didn't want to hear this conversation secondhand. Alex pressed the speaker button down so she could listen as well.

Larry's voice sounded oilier over the phone than in person as it floated into the room.

"I have some great news for you folks. If you weren't here in Vegas at this very moment, you wouldn't believe your luck."

Alex motioned to Stephanie to remain silent and let him handle their end of the conversation. He encouraged Larry to go on.

"A baby should be available toward the end of this week. It's a little girl. A newborn."

"That's wonderful," Alex crooned. "Just wonderful. My wife will be thrilled when I tell her."

"I'll come through on the particulars of where and when the exchange will be made just as soon as I finalize the paperwork with my immediate supervisor."

"I'll have your money ready by tomorrow," Alex

guaranteed. "How do hundred-dollar bills work for you?"

"Just fine." One could almost visualize the drool dripping off the man's chin as he assured Alex that he would "be in touch sometime tomorrow."

By the time the call was disconnected, Stephanie was shivering in a pool of her own sweat. A still-naked Alex enfolded her in his arms and proceeded to state the obvious.

"You're wet, honey. Here, let me dry you off."

He took the towel from her and proceeded to rub her down. That he grew hard in the process did not impede his efficiency, and Stephanie began to thaw beneath his gentle ministrations.

"Thank you," she said between teeth that chattered slightly despite the balmy temperature of the room.

Alex wrapped her up in one of the hotel's fluffy complimentary bathrobes.

"We'll have to act fast," Alex told her. "Since Natalie has already run off with a baby that they planned on selling, and isn't about to offer up her child as a pawn in this sick game, we have to find a way of getting some incriminating evidence before another poor woman loses her baby. I hate to scare you, but I think you should know that things are heating up back home."

Stephanie couldn't imagine them being any warmer there than they were here. "What do you mean?"

"I spoke to Darin ibn Shakir back at the Club earlier today. He had some very bad news to relate. It seems that Dr. Birkenfeld was in police custody for a short while, but an unfortunate accident allowed him to escape. Since he's somehow managed to elude the local authorities in Royal, I'm guessing that he's holed up here in Vegas. He's probably the supervisor Larry was referring to.''

Not wanting to scare her any more than was absolutely necessary to ensure her own safety, Alex didn't add that a Dr. Birkenfeld was also likely the murderer who had killed the real Dr. Beldon. The intent of this mission was to put the entire ring out of business once and for all, and that meant getting the goods on Birkenfeld. Larry Sutter was a relatively small fish in these polluted waters.

Until then, Alex vowed to remain vigilant for any sign of Birkenfeld lurking in the shadows. He had little doubt that the man was close by. His Cattleman's sources were operating under the assumption that Birkenfeld was running not only from the police but also from some nefarious loan sharks. The fact that Natalie had absconded with a huge chunk of the money he could have used to pay off his debts surely left him in a desperate predicament.

''If you're telling me this to scare me, it's working,'' Stephanie admitted, glancing nervously over her shoulder. ''But don't worry. I'm as committed to seeing this whole thing out as you are. I doubt if anything could be harder on me than today's performance. Just tell me what you want me to do tomorrow and trust me not to let you down.''

Her choice of words stung. Once their mission was over, Alex feared that he would be the one to let this amazing, brave woman down. The thought pained him. He didn't know how exactly things had become so complicated in a relationship based on pure subterfuge, but over the course of a few days Stephanie had done something no other woman had ever managed to do before. That was to get under his skin. Leading her back to bed with the caveat that they both would need a good night's sleep to be in top form for whatever tomorrow threw at them, he knew only that things were about to get a whole lot more complicated yet. Tomorrow, the danger would be all too real.

Eleven

The day dawned bright against the desert horizon. Stephanie hadn't slept well, but she so loved the feeling of being in Alex's arms that she lay awake a long time reveling in the sensation of being wrapped in the protective cocoon of his strong, masculine body. Worried that her fidgeting would needlessly awaken him, she reluctantly left the warmth of the bed and rose to sit beside the window. There she pondered her future in the silence of a heart overflowing with rare self-pity.

Come what may, their little charade was drawing to a close, and life as she knew it as Alexander Kent's wife would be over. Stephanie twisted the ring on her finger so that it caught the rays of the morning sun and reflected them upon the walls of her gilded cage. Slipping the ring off her finger, she studied the many facets that so reminded her of Alex's personality and the tears she was determined to keep locked deep inside.

"I want you to keep it."

Those generous and yet cold words interrupted Stephanie's solitude. Propped up in bed on one elbow, disheveled and unshaven, Alex looked like an advertisement utilizing the raw elements of sex appeal to shamelessly peddle a product.

"I couldn't possibly," she assured him.

Though her voice quivered, the smile she gave him was as calm and steady as the one painted on the *Mona Lisa.* What was the point of telling him that every time she looked at that ring upon her finger, she felt a fraud. Their mockery of a marriage made a mockery of her feelings for him as well. Whether the offer was inspired by generosity or guilt, such a reminder was destined to bring her only certain misery.

"Come here, sweetheart." Alex patted the empty spot beside him. "We need to talk."

"About what?"

"Us."

Stephanie rose from her lonely, sunrise spot. Behind her, Vegas shimmered like a rosy mirage. Having reached her own conclusions about the impossibility of carrying forth their sham of a relationship beyond the tinsel of a town built upon fantasy, she was not about to lose the last shred of dignity to which she clung. She stood her ground a good arm's length away from the bed that tempted her to abandon her pride altogether.

''What about us?'' she asked in a voice more weary than anything else.

Silhouetted against the red rising sun, Stephanie willed her backbone to keep from collapsing.

''I've been thinking that there's no reason we can't continue like this after we return home.''

Alex's deep voice was as thick and sweet as honey straight from the comb. Hope welled up inside Stephanie's heart and flowed over her lips without giving any consideration to the impact it might have. Her eyes grew luminous. Her voice faltered.

''Are you proposing?''

The look of surprise that crossed Alex's face told Stephanie all she needed to know. She winced as he backpedaled all over her tender emotions.

''That's not exactly what I had in mind.''

The echo of those words hung over them like a dying sprig of mistletoe left over from a Christmas holiday past.

As painful as it was to face the truth, Stephanie did not shyly avert her eyes nor choose her words in regard to softening their impact. ''Let me get this straight. You want me to keep a ring symbolizing a commitment you're not ready to make, a ring likely made of glass intended to fool the whole world into believing that we—''

A muscle in Alex's jaw jumped.

''It's real enough.''

''The diamond or the fidelity it's meant to symbolize?''

''Don't be coy,'' Alex snapped, splaying a hand through his hair in a gesture that Stephanie had come to recognize as a sure sign of his frustration. "I'm talking about that rock on your hand. Regardless of how things work out between us, I want you to have it."

Stephanie wasn't particularly surprised that Alex would dismiss the possibility of marriage out of hand, but she was hurt that he would lump her into the same category as other women he had known who could be bought with expensive trinkets. Most would jump at the chance of sharing his bed on whatever terms he set forth.

"Without the benefit of marriage, the ring doesn't mean much, does it?"

"You can hardly expect me to make that kind of commitment!" Alex exclaimed.

Where his words were a loud explosion of anger, Stephanie's were soft with understanding.

"I never have expected anything from you."

Looking as if he had just been hit over the head by a bag of wet cement, Alex strained to insert a note of patience into his voice.

"I've come to care a great deal for you, Stephanie, and I would very much like to continue seeing you once this job is over."

"Seeing me on the side, you mean?"

Had Stephanie a tissue in her hand, she would have spit those ugly words into it and disposed of them in the nearest garbage can.

There was a sneer on Alex's face as he posed the question, "I suppose you were expecting a mutually exclusive relationship?"

"I already told you I'm not expecting anything

from you—other than that you treat me with some dignity until we accomplish what we set out to do here.''

It came as no shock that Alex wouldn't want to give up the carefree lifestyle he'd enjoyed before he'd known her. Stephanie *was* surprised, however, that he wanted to continue seeing her when their mission was completed and he was under no obligation to pretend. If she were the kind of woman who was into playing mind games, she might have tried pressing her advantage. But Stephanie was as straightforward as the arrow Cupid had shot from his bow to cleave her poor heart in two.

Unlike Alex, she was ready to give up the best thing that had ever happened to her without a protest. If he would only allow her to hold on to her pride, she could come out of this relationship with something far more valuable than a fabulous diamond ring. In exchange for her heart, Alex had given her a sense of self-respect and belief in herself that had been missing from her previous life. Whatever obstacles life put in front of her in the future, she could always fall back on her memories of the time they'd spent together.

She lifted her proud chin in the air. A woman who could transform herself into a femme fatale in less than two weeks surely was entitled to more than the bread crumbs at life's banquet. As tempting as it was to accept any terms he offered, she would not be his mistress.

''I think it would be best if we went our separate ways once this is over,'' she told him. ''You have to know that it's not going to be easy for me to pick up the threads of a life that's so very dull in comparison to the one you've introduced me to. It'll be hard enough explaining to my students, not to mention the school board and my principal, why I faked a marriage to the most notorious playboy in Texas without further jeopardizing my virtue by continuing a dead-end relationship that is ultimately just going to leave me feeling bad about myself.''

''To hell with what people think!'' he snapped. ''You never have to work another day in your life if you don't want to.''

On a certain level, Stephanie was flattered that Alex wanted to keep on seeing her. On another, it was purely insulting. He reminded her of a spoiled child being denied a toy. Wishing there was some way she could make him understand how offensive his proposition was, Stephanie sat on the edge of the bed. She reached out and cupped his chin in one hand.

His morning stubble pricked her skin, making her feel soft and feminine by comparison. She placed a kiss upon his cheek, trying to memorize his natural scent.

''I can pretend to be your wife for a few days because our cause is so very worthy, but I could never agree to becoming your mistress. Surely you understand why.''

The thunderous look on Alex's face told her that he wasn't interested in her reasoning. It occurred to Stephanie that this was probably the closest he had ever come to offering any woman a commitment. She had never seen him so angry. Or so vulnerable.

"Because you think you can get more out of me as my wife than my lover?" he demanded. "So you can hamstring me financially and blackmail me emotionally if I were stupid enough to be the kind of man my father was—one so desperate to fill the hole that my mother left in our lives that he let a string of gold diggers try to fill it?"

Rather than drawing away from that terrible outburst, Stephanie took Alex's magnificent head into her lap. Never before had she glimpsed the hurt little boy peeking out from behind those sharp green eyes. It had never occurred to her that Alex avoided commitment because he had been deeply wounded in the past. She had been so worried that he would discard her without a second thought that she had accepted his playboy facade at face value.

"I'm sorry," she said, pressing for no more than he was willing to give of his own volition.

"My mother left both of us behind with less compunction than most people would abandon a couple of stray cats," Alex told her.

After all these years, the pain was still raw in his voice. Stephanie suspected it was the first time he'd ever bared his soul like that to another human being, and it was a tribute to his faith in her that he allowed her to continue holding him.

Soft light filtered into the room, casting a halo around the man who had just asked her to do something totally against her character. That he was flawed did not compromise her love for him. His hair was dark silk beneath her fingers. His heart a broken plaything.

"Not all women are like that," she murmured.

Stephanie couldn't imagine a mother abandoning her child. The fact that Alexander would make such a fine father himself made her grieve for lost opportunity.

"Some women would rather die than to give up a child," she added.

Her thoughts went to Natalie Perez. How incredibly brave she had been to steal her baby back from the dangerous men who they themselves were here to catch.

"I know you don't want to hear it again, but it bears repeating," Stephanie said, continuing to caress his hair. "I love you completely. I don't have any trouble telling you that. You're the one who can't seem to bring yourself to tell me the same."

When he bucked in her arms, she put her index finger to his lips and bade him hear her out.

"It would be wrong of me to ask you to say something you don't mean, so I won't. No one expects someone as glamorous and worldly as you to commit to someone as down-to-earth and old-fashioned as me. I can respect that."

Alex sputtered at her choice of words, but the unshed tears in Stephanie's eyes demanded no less of him than he allow her to finish her thoughts without interruption.

"In return, I need you to respect me. Just because other women might be happy with any arrangement you set up, you can't expect me to jump in and out of your bed at your convenience. I know it's an old line, but it's true. I'm not that kind of a girl. Trust me on this, darling,'' she said, pausing to place a feather-light kiss upon his forehead. ''In the long run, it wouldn't be good for either of us.''

Alex sighed in exasperation. One could hardly argue against the virtue that set Stephanie apart from every other woman who had ever tried to use him. Her lack of tears and recriminations left him at a loss to rouse the kind of righteous indignation that had served him so well in past breakups. His voice was flat and unemotional when he finally responded.

''Have it your way then. The ring is yours regardless. A souvenir, so to speak.''

Stephanie wasn't up for arguing. She was too drained to tell him that she didn't need anything so flashy to remind her of their time together. What she really needed was something to help her forget it. Not sure if her heart would allow her to continue living and breathing without him, she wondered if she'd just made the biggest mistake of her life.

''For what it's worth,'' Alex told her, ''I've let a lot of women into my bed, but you're the first one I've ever let into my heart.''

Stephanie turned her head away so that he would not see her tears. The admission was as close to a declaration of love as she ever expected to hear from him. It was a sweet balm for a heart left battered and bruised upon the shores of loneliness.

The sound of the telephone ringing gave Stephanie the opportunity to wipe away her tears as Alex left the bed to answer the call of duty. As he predicted, it was Larry.

"Here in the hotel lobby is perfect, but seven o'clock works better for us than six."

Stephanie was amazed at how casual the conversation sounded. Anyone just walking into the room would think Alex was discussing the details of some legitimate business contract rather than the exchange of a baby stolen from its rightful mother and sold to the highest bidder.

"I'll have one hundred twenty-five thousand dollars wired to me today. I understand your need to have that amount in cash. Will a briefcase suffice?"

A long pause left Stephanie wondering why fate had conspired to cast her in such a nefarious plot. Shakespeare himself would have been challenged to come up with a more twisted scheme to throw two more opposite people together.

"Since I doubt babies are allowed inside the casino, I suggest that we sign the paperwork in the hotel restaurant."

There was another pause before Alex clarified. "Yes, the Eureka. I'll make a reservation there for seven o'clock under my name. Will anyone else be accompanying you?"

During yet another pause, Stephanie forgot to breathe. Although this was the moment they had been so desperately hoping for, it was hard to believe it was upon them.

"All right, I'll look for both of you then."

With that, Alex hung up the phone. He turned to Stephanie and filled her in on the details.

"We give them the money. They give us some paperwork and hand over the baby. It's that simple."

Stephanie couldn't bite back the bitter laugh that rose in her throat. "Simple," she repeated, feeling utterly hollow.

She stared at the ring on her finger. Nothing in that phone call was any more frightening than knowing that Alex didn't love her enough to make any but a sexual commitment to her. She offered him her heart upon a silver platter, and in return he offered nothing but baubles. That she saw the ring on her finger as nothing more than an attempt to buy her off and assuage his guilt should make it that much easier to give it up when the time came. Despite his insistence that she keep the ring, Stephanie didn't want it.

Bullets lost their edge to hurt her any more than Alex already had. If death were to come from this ill-fated mission, Stephanie couldn't help but feel it would be a blessing.

As hard as Alex pretended to be blasé about her decision to break off their relationship, he was secretly furious. In the past, he had treated his romantic relationships as expendable. With Stephanie it was an entirely different matter. Over the past few days his feelings for her had grown right along with his respect—exponentially. The truth was, he'd never met a more courageous, intelligent woman in his life. Her unique sense of humor could coax genuine belly laughs from him, her sincerity was as refreshing as drinking from the fountain of youth, and her sweetness both in and out of the bedroom was nothing short of addictive. Above all, Alex liked the way he felt when he was around her. Seeing himself reflected in those soft doe eyes of hers made him feel like the most wonderful man alive.

Giving up that feeling wasn't going to be easy.

That he couldn't convince Stephanie to accept their relationship on his terms didn't lessen his resolve to protect her as they entered the most precarious stage of their mission. If anything, it reinforced it. It was going to be twice as hard safeguarding a woman of virtue. Alex's FBI experience taught him that idealists were unpredictable creatures who were far more likely to take stupid risks in the name of principle than people who had the good sense to make their own welfare a top priority.

An earlier conversation with Sheikh Darin ibn Shakir left little doubt in his mind that Dr. Birkenfeld was growing more and more desperate by the minute. Since desperate men were known to take desperate measures, Alex's concern about Stephanie's safety was well founded. The thought of anything happening to her made his stomach ball up into a tight fist. He wondered if it was possible that his loss of objectivity might jeopardize their mission.

He proceeded to lay out the plan for the rest of the day with a precision designed to bolster Stephanie's nerves—if not his own.

"First we go downtown and pick up the money that Darin's wiring us from the Club."

Alex smiled bleakly.

"I hope you enjoy the irony as much as I do, knowing that the cool five hundred thousand dollars stashed away in the Cattlemen's safe for just this very purpose is the same money that Natalie stole from the very people with whom we're about to do business.''

Stephanie nodded, taking grim satisfaction in the news before offering up her own thoughts on the subject.

''Hopefully that money can eventually be used to ensure that all the stolen babies are reunited with their grieving mothers as well as to help facilitate proper adoptions for any couple who unknowingly played a part in this shady operation.''

''First things first,'' Alex reminded her.

Having played the part of a doting husband who wanted to give his wife a child at any cost gave him a broader perspective on such a couple's despair as well. Still, just because Stephanie's big heart went out to everyone involved in this sticky web didn't mean they could afford to get ahead of themselves.

''I moved our meeting with Larry to seven o'clock specifically because I want every employee in the adoption agency out of the building when we break into it.''

Stephanie offered no protest to this revelation beyond a wry observation. ''What's breaking and entering added to my growing list of criminal activities?''

Since her heart itself had just been broken into and vandalized at will, she was, at the moment feeling too numb to worry about a little thing like her own personal safety.

Alex gave her an encouraging smile.

''I knew I could count on you. Quitting time should be no later than five o'clock this afternoon. That gives us less than two hours to gain entry to the office and gather the documentation that will prove beyond a shadow of a doubt that Dr. Birkenfeld is illegally supplying the agency with stolen babies.''

''Piece of cake.''

Though Alex thought it said a great deal about Stephanie's character that she could be so flippant in the face of grave personal danger, he rued the day he'd talked her into participating in such a perilous scheme. The kind of people who stole babies from defenseless young women wouldn't hesitate to kill anyone who got in their way. And as much as he despised the thought of putting Stephanie in the line of fire, he also knew it was too late to back out now without risking the entire outcome of their mission.

When Alex had signed on as a member of the Texas Cattleman's Club he had taken an oath to uphold their motto of ''Leadership, Justice and Peace.'' He truly believed that the words emblazoned upon the iron-studded sign hanging over the entryway of their sanctum were worth risking his life for in the line of duty. He did not believe, however, that Stephanie should be subject to the same level of risk.

He reached under the bed and pulled out a black carrying case that was approximately the size of a school lunch box. Sliding the fasteners on each side of the handle open, Alex set the container upon his lap. Noting Stephanie's gasp as he opened the lid, he gave her an apologetic smile.

''No point in taking any unnecessary chances,'' he said. ''As the Boy Scouts like to say, one should always be prepared.''

Nestled inside the container upon a bed of egg crate-shaped black foam were a small black gun and two clips. No bigger than the extension of Alex's hand, the pistol looked more like a toy than an actual weapon. The Glock .40 weighed no more than a couple of pounds. He checked to make sure the gun and all the clips were fully loaded, then pointed the pistol at the wall. A tiny red dot appeared upon the white textured surface.

"What do you think you're doing?" Stephanie demanded to know.

"Making sure the laser sight is functional."

Though horror was evident in her eyes, she did her best to make light of a situation over which she no longer had any control.

"I'll never be able to use a laser light in a library lecture again," she said. Up until now she had only considered them a nuisance in the hands of mischievous children.

"How did that get in here?" she asked.

"I didn't smuggle it on board the airplane if that's what you're thinking. Suffice it to say, the Cattleman's Club is very well connected. It helps to have friends all over the country."

Though Alex had hoped to put his partner's mind at ease by letting her see how well protected she was, his efforts appeared to have the opposite effect upon her.

Her legs went suddenly wobbly beneath her, and Stephanie reached for the edge of the bed. She looked at Alex as if she were trapped with a madman in some surreal dream.

"Do you really think a gun is necessary?"

The expression on Alex's face spoke for itself. Dead serious about the task at hand, he strapped on a shoulder harness and put the pistol next to his heart. Then he slipped a jacket on. Had Stephanie not known what was beneath it, she would never have guessed he was packing heat.

"Don't forget to grab the list," he told her, trying to take her mind off his firearm.

He was referring, of course, to the record of names that Natalie had cross-referenced back when she had worked for Dr. Birkenfeld—before she surmised what a monster he really was. As mindlessly as a robot, Stephanie did as she was told.

"It'll all be over soon," Alex reassured her.

He longed to take her in his arms and make her forget the ugliness of their situation by kissing her completely senseless, but he restrained himself. She had made it perfectly clear that once their mission was over, so was their relationship. He refused to be blackmailed into marriage. His old man had taught him that particular lesson all too well before passing on and leaving four ex-wives clamoring over the estate he'd left entirely to his only son.

"Very soon," Stephanie repeated dully, reaching for the tiny microphone that she would wear at tonight's final rendezvous with fate.

Hearing that, Alex couldn't help but assume she was eager to get back to a life that wasn't fraught with the dangers of tracking underworld criminals— or laying her heart on the line for a man who didn't deserve to kiss her feet. What he didn't know was

that her brave facade hid the dread of returning to a
life that would be empty without him.

After picking up the money that the Texas Cattleman's Club wired them, they proceeded to stake out
the office where Larry was busily typing up false
adoption papers and thinking about how he was going
to spend his share of the cash he'd be collecting in a
short couple of hours. A couple wearing earnest faces
was leaving just as Stephanie and Alex pulled up.
They parked a safe distance away to avoid detection.

"You know, if we're successful, couples just like
us will be forced to give up babies they've come to
love as their own."

Alex sighed. Stephanie's words carried a weight of
responsibility that he refused to accept.

"It's not up to us to play God, Steph. Our job is
to right a great wrong. You can take some consolation
from the fact that Natalie made off with over half a
million dollars from these scoundrels that can be used
to reunite babies with their rightful mothers and also
to help couples like us use means to adopt a child
legally."

Stephanie took what comfort she could from his
words. Both of them were surprised and aggravated
by the work ethic that had Larry locking up the place
a half hour after the end of a regularly scheduled
workday. At 5:33, he left the building with a blond
bombshell hanging on his elbow. Alex scoped the
twosome out using a diminutive pair of high-powered
binoculars. The woman had some dry cleaning draped
over her free arm. When she hung it up in the back

of Larry's gray Lexus, it revealed itself to be a white uniform.

"What do you want to bet she's playing the part of the nurse Larry promised to bring along to tonight's meeting?"

"Bad casting," Stephanie muttered, turning a critical eye to the woman she secretly dubbed Nurse Goodbody. If memory served her right, this was the same receptionist who had made her feel so transparent during their first visit to this office.

They waited only long enough to make sure the place was deserted before Alex suggested they take a walk around to the back of the building. Stephanie felt as if she should be wearing a black ski mask and matching cat-burglar suit instead of a pair of dark slacks and a blazer. Taking a small case from his pocket, Alex proceeded to pick the lock with the kind of quick precision that led Stephanie to believe this wasn't his first attempt at breaking and entering. A moment later the door swung open.

Stephanie produced a list of names and dates from her purse as Alex switched on the computer. While he attempted to break into the electronic files, she started rifling through a metal file cabinet. That process took far less time than one would anticipate. The number of files on hand was surprisingly small, but if any of the infants' footprints upon the birth certificates Stephanie collected matched those on the death certificate given to Natalie Perez when she was told her baby had not survived its birth, it would provide the concrete evidence the authorities needed to shut down the ring for good and put the perpetrators behind bars for the rest of their natural lives. The fact that Alex was having trouble getting into the system led them both to believe that was where the goods were.

"Check the desk drawers and look for anything that might be a log-in and password," Alex said, checking his watch.

Could the answer be staring her right in the face? Stephanie studied the only photograph in the room that didn't prominently feature Larry's family. In it, he had his arm around the shoulders of a smiling buddy who had apparently liked the picture so much that he had signed and dated it in the corner.

"Didn't you say that Birkenfeld's first name was Roman?"

"Uh-huh," Alex replied, still intent on his quest.

A queasy feeling came over Stephanie as she studied the boat in front of which the picture had been taken. Could anyone really be so callous that they would actually brag about purchasing a luxury sailboat from the proceeds of stolen babies? The arrogance of such a subliminal boast indicated just how sick a man Roman Birkenfeld was.

"Try *R.B.'s Baby*," she suggested, offering him the name painted on the boat.

"Bingo!"

Stephanie couldn't draw her gaze away from that disturbing photograph. "If we don't come up with something concrete soon, I'm afraid the good doctor will be out of the office indefinitely—and hard to reach once he sets sail for the high seas and world-class luxury ports of call."

The sound of computer keys tapping at a frenzied clip beneath Alex's fingers reiterated his sense of urgency. Unfortunately, none of the names on Natalie's list were leading anywhere but to frustration. Alex ran a hand through his dark hair and checked his watch for the fourth time in five minutes.

"Unfortunately, their files are more complicated than their back door," Alex muttered. He pierced Stephanie with his gaze. "We can't take a chance on being late to tonight's appointment. If they smell a skunk, the whole operation could be jeopardized."

"That leaves us only two options," she responded with the kind of logic and grit that Alex had come to expect of her. "Either you go back to the hotel and meet with Larry and his nurse and stall until I can get there with the goods, or I do. What's your preference?"

I'd prefer to turn back the hands of time and nullify anything I had to do with involving you in this whole ugly mess, he thought miserably.

His decision ultimately had nothing to do with whom he thought was the better actor. Alex simply would not consider leaving Stephanie alone with Larry under any circumstances. Thinking she would be far safer interfacing with a computer than with known criminals, he chose the former of her two suggestions.

"I'll go back to the hotel restaurant and tell them you're out shopping for last minute baby items to make the trip home as comfortable as possible. At a quarter to seven, there will be a cab waiting to meet you at the stoplight at the end of the block. Whether you've located anything incriminating or not, you will be in that cab and headed back to the hotel. Hopefully Larry'll be excited enough about receiving a briefcase with over a hundred thousand in cool cash that he won't worry if you show up a little late.''

Stephanie urged Alex to give up his seat in front of the screen before time betrayed them both. ''As a librarian, I know a few things about computers myself. In seedier circles, I'm known as the scourge of interlibrary loans.''

Alex balked. ''I don't have a good feeling about this. I hate leaving you alone and—''

''Go on,'' Stephanie told him. ''While I'm copying the files, you can be signing the paperwork that should put these SOB's behind bars for life, which is what we're here to do. Don't waste another minute of precious time worrying about me. I'll be fine.''

''I'll leave my cell phone on in case anything goes wrong. You do the same,'' he insisted, unwilling to cut off all communication completely.

Stephanie's courage was enough to bring Alex to his knees. Why he ever thought he could live the rest of his life without this woman was as silly as thinking one could make a computer work without electricity. He had every intention of telling her that, of setting the record straight and having it out with his own heart—just as soon as this nasty business was behind them.

Now, however, was not the time to tarry. Not when a baby's life was on the line and time was quickly running out.

Twelve

Stephanie had a full half of the computer files copied when she heard the back door open. Thinking it was Alex, she started to call out to him, but a high-pitched giggle paralyzed her before she could open her mouth.

"Sorry I got you so distracted that you forgot your paperwork. I'm so happy that Roman's cut of the deal should be enough to get the loan sharks off his back."

"If only he'll use it for that…"

Stephanie recognized the second voice as Larry's. Before shutting off the light switch, she glanced at the computer screen.

68% copied

"I'm afraid my old friend's propensity for gambling is matched only by his propensity for violence. And both have compromised our business arrangement. Just so you know, this will be my final favor to my old college buddy. After tonight, I'm done.''

''I can't imagine you pulling the plug on such a sweet, lucrative deal. Surely you don't plan on maintaining the lifestyle to which your wife and family have become accustomed by chasing after ambulances again.''

''No need to, Mary,'' Larry replied dryly. ''My days as a working-stiff contingency lawyer are over. It's too bad that Perez woman threw a monkey wrench into this operation, but she did. If Roman knows what's good for him, he'll cut his losses and get out while the getting's good.''

Stephanie took a quick look at the computer screen and tried to force air into her lungs in deep enough breaths that she didn't risk hyperventilating. The voices outside the door were becoming more distinct the closer they came.

87% copied

''What he's planning on doing is cutting that Perez bitch's throat and getting back all the money from the last botched job. I'd hate to be her when Roman gets his hands on her. I bet he'll make her suffer before he kills her.''

Stephanie's hand went to her own throat, and she felt her heart beating there. The green glow of the computer turned her hands a ghastly shade.

100% copied

She snapped the computer switch off and grabbed for the disk at the same time.

''If he knows what's good for him, he'll pay off those loan sharks and hightail it out of the country before anyone connects him with the death of Dr. Belden. The smartest thing he could do is sail around the world and into anonymity—just as I intend to do.''

Larry's voice was just outside the door. Stephanie ducked beneath the desk and began frantically digging through her purse for her cell phone, when the door swung open. She froze, afraid to so much as breathe too loudly.

''I left the stuff right on your desk.'' The woman sounded petulant. ''Of course, considering what we were doing on it just before leaving, I suppose I'll have to forgive you knocking the paperwork on the floor.''

Stephanie worried that the sound of her heart beating out of control would draw them to her hiding place. Beneath her left knee was the piece of paperwork that they had come back to retrieve. In the waning evening light filtering through the window, she could see the distinct imprint of a baby's foot pressed in black ink against the white sheet of paper.

She pushed it as far away from her as she could without drawing attention to the act and tried to make herself as small as she could beneath Larry's desk—and makeshift bed.

''There it is,'' Mary squealed, spying the paper on the floor.

Stephanie had only a partial view of the woman as she bent down to pick it up. Her ample bosom almost brushed against the floor.

''Are you sure we don't have time for a quickie

before we head to the Eureka?'' she offered with a purr.

Stephanie tried to keep from gagging on the woman's perfume, which was applied with such excess it permeated the air all around her.

''It is safe to say, my dear, that our relationship is over. When Roman arrives to pick up his share of the money, I intend to deliver you into his competent hands as well. Seeing how he's under the assumption you and he are an exclusive item, it would be in both of our interests to keep our private affairs—er—private from him. See if you can't convince Roman to get out of Vegas as quickly as possible. Once our young couple arrive at the nursery and discover there is no infant awaiting them, there's no telling what they might do.''

''It's your loss,'' Mary sniffed, clearly more perturbed by his rejection than scared of the consequences.

''Trust me. We'd best not be late for our appointment. Our client doesn't strike me as the kind of man used to waiting on anybody. We'd better get going.''

Stephanie's muscles were cramping, but she didn't dare move, and only chanced tiny sips of air. Had she ever envisioned herself crouching under a desk hiding from the kind of people who relished the idea of slitting a young woman's throat, she doubted she would have ever accepted this mission when Alex first broached the subject. She had a clear view of two sets of feet as they turned and headed toward the door. The fact that Larry's shoes could use a good polish was indicative of the pinch Natalie's stunt had put on their operation. From the conversation she had just overheard, Stephanie suspected that while Larry was ready to get out while he could, Roman Birkenfeld was intent on revenge. Indeed, Alex's fears were not at all unfounded. As Birkenfeld was on the loose, Natalie was in danger.

From her odd vantage point, Stephanie could see the door open. She almost wept at the sight. As it clicked shut, she began to shake uncontrollably at the realization that she was safe.

It was at that exact moment that the cell phone in her purse went off.

Something was terribly wrong. Long before his watch confirmed the fact, premonition settled into Alex's bones and made him anxious. The fact that Stephanie didn't answer her cell phone was enough to propel him out of his seat. Pacing the length of the restaurant, he looked as dangerous as a caged bear. One whose bite was far worse than his growl.

''Where are they?'' he snarled to no one in particular.

If Larry and his nurse didn't show up in exactly one minute, Alex was going to have to choose between salvaging this mission or going back for Stephanie. He was out the door well before that minute was up.

Chosen for this assignment by his peers because of his ability to remain calm under duress, Alex blanched when he saw Larry's Lexus parked in front of the adoption service. It hadn't taken him long to get there from the hotel, which he had expressly based on its proximity to the agency itself. He hit the front door of the brick building running. That it wasn't locked only intensified his apprehension as he made his way down a dark hallway to where he had last left Stephanie.

The sight of her gagged and bound to a chair caused him to go nearly blind with rage. Her microphone dangled loose from a shirt that had been ripped at the collar. It hung open revealing more than Alex wanted anyone else in the world to see of the woman he loved. Her eyes widened when she saw him. Never before had reason and restraint abandoned him at the same time. It was a frightening thing to behold. It took all his strength to restrain himself from rushing in and freeing her without stopping to assess the situation.

"What should we do with her now?" asked the blonde leaning her weight against Larry's desk. Her shrill voice drew blood-red nails over Alex's exposed nerves.

"How should I know?"

Pressing himself against the wall, Alex inched forward. So embedded was his FBI training into every fiber of his being that he didn't even have to think about his next move.

"Let's just find Roman. He'll know what to do. He'll probably be thrilled to have a hostage drop right into his lap."

Larry's voice rose with his sense of growing panic. "This is getting way out of hand. I never agreed to participate in kidnapping."

Mary's laughter mocked him. "Do you think it's the stork that's been dropping those babies off on your front door?"

"Shut up!"

Counting on their tension to provide a one-second cover, Alex burst into the room with his gun drawn. The woman's shriek pierced the air. Larry swore and stepped behind Stephanie. She was in no position to do anything but try to communicate with her eyes to Alex that she was more frightened than hurt. The swelling across her cheek where Larry had slapped her left a mark but didn't look as if it had caused any serious damage.

Larry's sense of self-preservation kicked in as his hands encircled Stephanie's slender neck.

"Throw down your gun, and I won't be tempted to snap your pretty little wife's neck in two," he snarled.

"Move away from her, and I won't kill you," Alex countered.

The blood drained from Larry's face.

"It's over," Alex told him. "If you cooperate with the police, you might actually stand a chance of getting some leniency in the courts. A smart lawyer like you shouldn't have any trouble turning state's evidence into a reduced sentence. We really want Birkenfeld, not you—or you."

Alex pointed his gun at the blonde. "The two of you are in serious trouble, but nothing worth dying for. Why don't you tell your friend here to give it up. Tell him it's over."

Not one to be moved by reason, the woman screamed, ''Kill her while you've got the chance!''

Larry's hands slipped from Stephanie's neck to the edge of her chair. Wrenching it sideways, he tipped it over and made a dash for the back door. The sharp edge of the desk caught Stephanie on the side of the head just before everything went black.

Mary ran in the opposite direction. The sound of a police siren outside did not dissuade Alex from his pursuit of Larry. When Stephanie failed to answer her phone, he had dialed 911. He suspected this so-called nurse would be collecting her first-class ride to the police station shortly.

Alex concerned himself with not letting Larry escape. He had no doubt that the lawyer would roll over on his own mother if it meant reducing any time he spent in the big house. For the first time in his life, Alex was out for revenge. The handprint on Stephanie's face stirred a sense of vengeance in him that he had hitherto never known.

Alex leaped over the desk and gave chase. In less than a dozen steps, he caught up to the frantic attorney grappling with a doorknob. Cornered, he turned and threw a wild punch. Alex deflected it with a martial arts move that shattered the lawyer's glass chin with the heel of his left foot. The focused strength of that single catlike movement took Larry completely by surprise. His head snapped backward as he hit the wall, and he began a slow slide to the floor.

It was over almost before it started.

Stephanie came to in Alex's arms. He was looking at her with such concern reflected in his eyes that she almost thought she was dreaming. Her head hurt something fierce, and it took her a while to realize that the blood trickling down his arm was hers.

"Before you even think about passing out again, I have something important to ask you," Alex told her.

"The disk is in my purse," she mumbled, jumping to an assumption that made her head throb all the more. "Wherever that is."

Slowly she became aware of police officers milling around and an EMT anxiously peering over Alex's shoulder.

"Forget the damn disk. It's you I'm worried about."

The frustration in his voice was off set by the tender way he cradled her against his body. The sound of his heart beating calmed her. Stephanie wished she could stay there forever and foreswear the stretcher they were bringing into the room for her.

"If I die now, I die a happy woman," she told him honestly.

Alex captured her hand in his as she reached up to sweep his hair away from his forehead. She was relieved to see nary a scratch upon that handsome face.

"Don't talk like that. You're not going to die," he said with such intensity that one could imagine him wrestling with the Angel of Death to keep him away from her.

"You can continue this touching scene on the way to the hospital," the EMT interjected.

"One more minute," Alex snapped, giving the burly fellow a warning glance that would have stopped an army in its tracks.

"The question I want to ask you is…"

He paused to look so deeply into her eyes that Stephanie suspected he could see her soul's reflection shimmering there.

"Will you marry me?"

Stephanie felt herself grow so light-headed she was afraid she really would die before she could answer him. She wondered if she was delirious. Weakly she lifted her hand and directed his attention to the ring on her finger.

"Only if it's for real this time."

Alex managed to get in one good kiss before the EMT muscled him out of the way and loaded his fiancée into the waiting ambulance.

Epilogue

Green-velvet curtains closed on a sold-out show. Applause echoed in the Royal High School Theater, and a few people were actually moved to dig tissues and handkerchiefs out of their pockets. Granted most were parents and relatives of members of the cast. Still in all, the student actors did a wonderful job portraying their characters. At least, as Stephanie was likely to point out, they all knew their lines, where they were supposed to be onstage at any given moment, and spoke loudly enough that they could be heard in the back of the theater. While not yet ready for Broadway, it was the most memorable Shakespearean production any of the audience could remember performed upon that venerable, if not rickety, old stage.

As the curtain opened one last time to reveal the

cast joined hand in hand, the audience rose to its feet and rendered a standing ovation. Risen from the dead, Romeo and Juliet shared a deep bow together. A diminutive diamond on Launa Beth's hand sparkled beneath the stage lights. It came as no surprise to anyone who knew them well that Launa had accepted Junior Weaver's proposal just before the curtain opened on tonight's show, and that they would go on to college together in the fall as man and wife.

As Shakespeare himself well knew, love wears many masks. The one Launa wore during the rehearsals preceding tonight's performance covered her true feelings for the one boy who could make her heart soar. Both Stephanie and Alex could relate. They came home to Royal minus the masks they had worn for years to protect their true identities from the outside world. A few short weeks ago, they had believed love to be little more than some letters cleverly arranged on page by a playwright hoping to sell tickets to his production. The idea of lovers actually willing to sacrifice their lives for one another was moving only in the abstract. Today, as Stephanie accepted a bouquet of roses from her grateful cast, she stepped upon the stage a new woman. The change in Royal's librarian was so dramatic that several people in the audience could be heard asking if the exquisite creature taking a bow was in fact the same Miss Firth that they only thought they knew.

Indeed, it was not.

That woman had exchanged her name and life with a deliriously happy Mrs. Alexander Kent. The wedding performed in Las Vegas before they returned home to Royal was legally binding and as real as the stunning ring on Stephanie's finger. Alex promised to follow up that civil ceremony performed by a justice of the peace with as extravagant a church wedding as his new bride wanted. She asked only for family and friends to join them in a simple ceremony to celebrate the beginning of their new life together.

An overly animated matron whose son played the part of Mercutio jabbed the fellow theatergoer in the seat next to her. "It's impossible to believe that's the same woman who catalogs books in the library."

"She is most beautiful," the man agreed, ignoring both the woman's sharp elbow to his ribs and her pointed jab.

Alex's old friend Sheikh Darin ibn Shakir looked out of place amid Royal's usual patrons of the arts. At six foot two the man gave off mysterious vibes that drew women's attention from every corner of the room. His dark hair was pulled back into a ponytail fastened with a leather thong, a single gold loop earring glistened against his dark complexion, and his goatee was neatly trimmed. Though he would have looked at home in traditional Middle Eastern clothing, tonight he was dressed all in black.

He seemed unaware of the interested glances he generated among the women in the crowd. He was here on business—unfinished business. He had every intention of pumping his good friend Alex for even the smallest detail that could help him track down

Birkenfeld and put the doctor behind bars for life. He planned to be in Vegas before morning.

A tearful director gestured for her husband to join her onstage. He did so reluctantly. As the final curtain closed, Stephanie was seen whispering in Alex's ear.

"Now that this production is behind us, I'd like to get started on a new one right away."

Alex looked perplexed.

"I thought you'd decided to turn in your notice at the end of the term."

Stephanie gave him an enigmatic smile and drew his hand to her stomach.

"I was thinking more along the lines of producing a baby of our own. Or maybe a whole passel to fill up that new house you bought me for a wedding present."

Alex's eyes snapped to hers, then widened in pleasure. Taking her in his arms, he whispered in her ear, "I've heard you're a demanding director. I suppose there will be lots of late-night rehearsals."

Recognizing that heavy-lidded look as lust, Stephanie responded in kind.

"We'd both have to agree to a grueling schedule," she agreed.

Though her voice was teasing, her brown eyes were as sincere as her desire to have his babies. The love she felt for her husband redoubled every day and could not be contained in a heart already so full that it flowed over. She looked at the man who had made all her once seemingly impossible dreams come true and tried to gauge how he felt about becoming a father. Stephanie had always wanted children, but without a husband, the idea seemed highly impractical. She hoped Alex's difficult childhood would not make him averse to starting a family of his own.

Alex's lips twitched in amusement.

"So where do I sign up?" he asked. "I would very much like to commit my considerable talents to such a production—on one condition."

Stephanie feigned an exaggerated sigh.

"And just what kind of prima donna demands is the star of my show making now?"

"Just that this production have a happy ending. No more tragedies—or near tragedies for this family."

Stephanie couldn't have agreed more. Having witnessed enough heartbreak to last her a lifetime, she was ready for the happily-ever-after that she'd been seeking for years in books and on the stage. While life might not tie up every loose end as the great bard did so masterfully, she was living proof that love truly can conquer all. And while it was also true that Dr. Birkenfeld was as of yet unaccounted for, with his accomplices Mary Campbell and Larry Sutter singing to the authorities like gilded canaries, Stephanie felt certain it wouldn't be long before the "good doctor" was behind bars as well. Alex's assurances that his Cattleman colleague Darin was on the case and would be headed for Vegas in the morning allowed them to plan an extended honeymoon free from worries of espionage, intrigue and danger.

For just as Launa and Junior would have to wait until after graduation to announce their engagement,

Dr. Birkenfeld's time would surely come. As Alex enveloped his wife in a passionate embrace and kissed her soundly to the applause of the assembled cast, Stephanie reveled in the knowledge that their happy ending was but a new and wonderful beginning of a script they would write together.

* * * * *

Don't miss the final installment of the
TEXAS CATTLEMAN'S CLUB:
THE STOLEN BABY

*Meet Darin Shakir—expert tracker and
brooding man of mystery. He's determined to
complete his mission on his own. But that's
before he winds up in Fiona Powers's
bed…and she finds her way into his heart!*

FIT FOR A SHEIKH
by Kristi Gold

*Coming to you from Silhouette Desire
in April 2004.*

*And now, for a sneak preview of
FIT FOR A SHEIKH,
please turn the page.*

One

Men viewed him as a dangerous loner who would stop at nothing in the search for justice. Women considered him a compelling lover who would stop at nothing in the pursuit of pleasure. A dark prince. Enigmatic. Invincible.

As a former military tracker, tempting fate and defying fear had become a way of life for Sheikh ibn Shakir. A means to escape his own demons and a noble legacy he had never embraced. Yet the mission he was about to undertake had resurrected past failures he'd rather forget. But he couldn't forget, not this time. Not until he saw the murderous Dr. Roman Birkenfeld—who had stolen infants from their mothers then sold them as if they were his to barter—punished for his heinous crimes. Whatever it might take.

Preparing for his departure to Las Vegas, Darin began to fill the black duffle bag with supplies and clothing he would need for his travels. He paused momentarily to survey the room where he'd resided over the past year. His cousin Hassim 'Ben' Rassad had welcomed him into his home and facilitated Darin's membership into the elite Texas Cattleman's Club, a group of men who assisted in apprehending criminals few would dare to confront. Although Darin was grateful for the opportunities, he planned to move on to the next mission alone, tracking an extremist in Obersburg who had threatened the royal family. He had no ties in America aside from his older brother, Raf, who resided in Georgia, and Ben. As for his homeland, Amythra, he'd vowed to never return. The place held nothing but bitter memories.

"The car is on its way."

Darin turned toward the door to find his cousin dressed in faded jeans and scuffed cowboy boots that gave no indication he, too, had been born into nobility. Glancing at the lone bag set on the end of the bed, Ben asked, "Is that all you are taking?"

"I don't anticipate remaining for more than a few days."

"You should pack this as well."

Darin afforded a cursory glance at the square of white cloth and gold band Ben held out to him. "I have no need for a *kaffiyeh* where I am going." He'd had no need for any royal trappings for some time now. Ben's brother, Kalib, ruled as king of Amythra, therefore Darin was far down the line in terms of inheriting the throne. A good thing because he did not want that burden. He never had.

Ben offered the *kaffiyeh* again. "You could use it as a disguise, if for no other reason."

Seeing no need to argue that point, Darin took the *kaffiyeh* from Ben and stuffed it inside the bag's outer pocket.

"Alexander Kent tells me he has arranged assistance from the Bureau," Ben said.

Something else that did not please Darin, although he greatly respected Alex Kent, a former FBI agent and fellow Cattleman's Club member. "I would prefer to work alone."

Ben released a frustrated sigh. "Might I remind you that when you joined our organization, you agreed to work with the others as a team?"

Darin needed no reminders. He'd been working that way for the past year, and he'd had no difficulty adhering to the policy. But this was different. This was personal. "I did not realize that this assignment would include other branches of law enforcement."

"It is necessary since this mission does not involve private hire. The illegal adoption ring and extortion violated federal law. That is the way in this country."

"I will honor the law. I will also have Birkenfeld in custody in a matter of days."

Ben looked skeptical. "Do you really believe you will find him so quickly?"

Darin holstered the Berretta, secured the strap over his shoulder then slipped a black jacket over his T-shirt and the gun. "Birkenfeld is not as smart as he believes, even if he did escape the authorities." And that thought brought about Darin's anger. He had been involved in the doctor's original capture, only to have the criminal slip through their hands due to Birkenfeld's cunning and desperation and one novice police officer's inadvertent mistake.

"Then you are certain he is still in Las Vegas?" Ben asked.

Normally Darin would be guarded with that information, something else he had pledged when he'd joined the Cattleman's Club. But Ben was still officially a member though he'd retired from active missions since his marriage. Therefore, Darin had no reason to withhold details in the case. "He is there, according to the attorney, Larry Sutter, Birkenfeld's cohort. Birkenfeld contacted Sutter on his cell phone and arranged a meeting in some obscure Las Vegas lounge. I am to join an operative posing as a bartender."

"This Sutter is in Las Vegas as well?"

"Yes, in a hospital under protective custody since he has decided to turn state's evidence in exchange for a lesser sentence. It appears he will be there for a while as he recovers from Kent's beating."

"Alexander Kent beat him?" Shock reflected in Ben's tone and expression.

"He was protecting his lover from Sutter while they were infiltrating the adoption ring. There are no limits to what a man will do for the woman he loves." Even kill if necessary, something Darin knew intimately.

Ben sent him a knowing look. "Very true. I, too, have been in that position."

So had Darin, yet he had failed where Ben had not.

Ben thrust his hands in his pockets and watched while Darin took a few more things from the bureau drawers and added them to the bag. Darin sensed his cousin wanted to say something more, and not necessarily anything he wanted to hear.

"Are you certain you should be the one undertaking this particular mission?" Ben asked, confirming Darin's suspicions.

"I volunteered. Unlike the other members involved, I have no wife with whom to be concerned." No one waiting for him. No one who really worried over his activities.

"It is past time for you to consider settling down, Darin. Past time you find a suitable woman to share in your life."

After stuffing the last of his clothing into the bag, Darin zipped it with a vengeance. "I have no desire to settle down. After Raf's wife died, I decided my brother and I are cursed when it comes to women."

Ben's smile was cynical. "I thought you were too logical to believe in curses."

"I was, before…" Before his world had come apart with the speed of a bullet.

"Before you lost her," Ben finished for him. "Yes, the outcome was tragic, but we are all fortunate, and grateful, that you stopped Habib before he did further harm. You had no control over the situation beyond that."

"I do not care to take the risk with another woman. Not with the life I choose to lead."

"Yet you risk your life much of the time. Why not

take a chance on finding a wife? I did, and I have no regrets.''

Darin recognized that Ben had found a very special woman. Someone worth that risk. An American woman whose determination and spirit equaled most men Darin had known. He could not blame his cousin for falling for Jamie. She was everything a man would desire in a life partner, beautiful and full of passion. Ben and Jamie's commitment and love for each other was obvious in every look they exchanged, a painful reminder of what Darin had once had—and lost—and the reason why he needed to leave their home. The other cried, ''Papa! Papa!'' as she rushed into the room and grabbed Ben around the legs, her light brown hair flowing over her tiny shoulders.

Ben picked up two-and-a-half-year-old Lena and lifted her high above his head, much to the little girl's delight. ''You are full of energy today, *yáahil*.'' He brought her into his arms and kissed her cheeks. ''I thought you were making *xúbuz* with your mother and Alima.''

Lena wrinkled her upturned nose. ''I don't like bread. I want cookies.'' She sent Darin a vibrant smile, much like her mother's, then pointed to his chin. ''Scratchies all gone, Dawin?'' she asked, as always mispronouncing his name, something Darin found endearing.

Ignoring the deep ache radiating from his heart, he rubbed his clean-shaven jaw and favored her with a smile. ''Yes, little one. All gone down the drain.'' He'd removed the goatee that morning to make himself less recognizable to Birkenfeld. He had also cut his hair to the top of his collar and now wore a gold loop in each ear. Hopefully enough of a change to disguise himself somewhat, which brought about a reminder of something he had almost forgotten.

Darin tucked his hair behind his ears and set the black baseball cap low on his forehead. He then picked up the bag and said, "I am ready."

Lena leveled her dark eyes on him. "Where ya goin', Dawin?"

He walked to her and ran a fingertip over her soft cheek. "To a place with many bright lights." And a man who needed to be tracked down and punished.

She leaned over and touched his jaw as if fascinated with the absence of whiskers. "I wanna go."

Darin took her hand and kissed her palm. "Not this time, little one."

As Darin, Ben and Lena headed through the great room, Jamie met them at the front door. "Leaving again, Darin?"

"For a time."

Jamie raked a hand through her blond hair and patted her distended abdomen. "I hope you'll be back in the next few days for the baby's birth. It's really something to see big tough Ben here in nervous father mode. I swear, I thought he was going to pass out when Lena—"

Ben halted her words with a kiss then wrapped his arm around her shoulder. "I was quite calm during Lena's birth."

Jamie grinned and Lena giggled. "If you say so, honey."

True affection passed between father, mother and

child, evident by shared smiles, Lena's head resting against Ben's chest, Jamie's arm around Ben's waist.

Needing to escape, Darin walked onto the porch, thankful to discover the sedan had arrived to take him to the airstrip. Seeing this closely bound family was almost too much for him to bear, although he would never reveal that to anyone.

Before entering the car, he turned to wave goodbye and little Lena, with her father's eyes and mother's smile, blew him a kiss.

Memories of what might have been crowded Darin's mind, save for one cruel bastard who had taken three lives—Ben's father, Darin's fiancée and their unborn child. A man much like Dr. Roman Birkenfeld. Both had no regard for the sanctity of life and the rare gift of love.

Darin vowed to hunt down Birkenfeld even if it proved to be his last act on earth. But in the process, Sheikh Darin ibn Shakir would not allow himself to feel his own pain. Not if he wanted to succeed.

You are about to enter the exclusive,
masculine world of the...

The Stolen Baby

Silhouette Desire's powerful miniseries features
six wealthy Texas bachelors—all members of the
state's most prestigious club—who must unravel
the mystery surrounding one tiny baby...and
discover true love in the process!

Available at your favorite retail outlet.

Silhouette®

Desire®

TEXAS Cattleman's Club

The Stolen Baby

A powerful miniseries featuring six wealthy Texas bachelors—all members of the state's most prestigious club—who set out to unravel the mystery surrounding one tiny baby... and discover true love in the process!

This newest installment continues with

FIT FOR A SHEIKH
by
Kristi Gold
(Silhouette Desire #1576)

Meet Darin Shakir—expert tracker and brooding man of mystery. He's determined to complete his mission on his own. But that's before he winds up in Fiona Powers's bed...and she finds her way into his heart!

Available March 2004 at your favorite retail outlet.

If you enjoyed what you just read,
then we've got an offer you can't resist!

Take 2 bestselling love stories FREE!

Plus get a FREE surprise gift!

Clip this page and mail it to Silhouette Reader Service™

IN U.S.A.
3010 Walden Ave.
P.O. Box 1867
Buffalo, N.Y. 14240-1867

IN CANADA
P.O. Box 609
Fort Erie, Ontario
L2A 5X3

YES! Please send me 2 free Silhouette Desire® novels and my free surprise gift. After receiving them, if I don't wish to receive anymore, I can return the shipping statement marked cancel. If I don't cancel, I will receive 6 brand-new novels every month, before they're available in stores! In the U.S.A., bill me at the bargain price of $3.57 plus 25¢ shipping and handling per book and applicable sales tax, if any*. In Canada, bill me at the bargain price of $4.24 plus 25¢ shipping and handling per book and applicable taxes**. That's the complete price and a savings of at least 10% off the cover prices—what a great deal! I understand that accepting the 2 free books and gift places me under no obligation ever to buy any books. I can always return a shipment and cancel at any time. Even if I never buy another book from Silhouette, the 2 free books and gift are mine to keep forever.

225 SDN DNUP
326 SDN DNUQ

Name	(PLEASE PRINT)	
Address	Apt.#	
City	State/Prov.	Zip/Postal Code

* Terms and prices subject to change without notice. Sales tax applicable in N.Y.
** Canadian residents will be charged applicable provincial taxes and GST.
All orders subject to approval. Offer limited to one per household and not valid to current Silhouette Desire® subscribers.
® are registered trademarks of Harlequin Books S.A., used under license.

DES02   ©1998 Harlequin Enterprises Limited

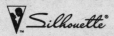

COMING NEXT MONTH

#1573 SCANDAL BETWEEN THE SHEETS—Brenda Jackson
Dynasties: The Danforths
There was one thing more seductive to hotshot reporter Jasmine Carmody than a career-making story: tall, dark businessman Wesley Brooks. But Wesley had his own agenda, and would do whatever it took to ensure Jasmine didn't uncover the scandal surrounding his close friends, the Danforths…even if it meant getting *closer* still to Jasmine!

#1574 KEEPING BABY SECRET—Beverly Barton
The Protectors
The sexual chemistry had been explosive between Lurleen "Leenie" Patton and Frank Latimer. And their brief but passionate affair had resulted in a baby…a son Frank knew nothing about. When tragedy struck and their child was kidnapped, Leenie needed Frank to help find their son. But first she had to tell Frank he was a father….

#1575 A KEPT WOMAN—Sheri WhiteFeather
Mixing business and pleasure was against the rules for U.S. Marshal Zack Ryder. But Natalie Pascal—the very witness he was supposed to be protecting—tempted him beyond reason. The vulnerable vixen hid from a painful past, and Zack told himself he was only offering her comfort with his kisses, his touch….

#1576 FIT FOR A SHEIKH—Kristi Gold
Texas Cattleman's Club: The Stolen Baby
Sheikh Darin Shakir was on a mission to find and bring to justice a dangerous fugitive who used Las Vegas as his playground. But unforeseen circumstances had left Darin with bartending beauty Fiona Powers as his Sin City tour guide. Together, they were hot on the trail of the bad guy…and getting even hotter for each other!

#1577 SLOW DANCING WITH A TEXAN—Linda Conrad
Making time for men was never a concern for workaholic Lainie Gardner. That is, until a scary brush with a stalker forced her into hiding. Now, deep in the wilderness with her temporary bodyguard, Texas Ranger Sloan Abbot, the sexual tension sizzled. Could Lainie give in to her deepest desires for the headstrong cowboy?

#1578 A PASSIONATE PROPOSAL—Emilie Rose
Teacher Tracy Sullivan had had a crash on surgical resident Cort Lander *forever*. But when the sexy single dad hired *her* on as his baby's nanny, things got a little more heated. Tracy decided that getting over her crush meant giving in to passion…but would a no-strings-attached affair pave the way for a love beyond her wildest dreams?

SDCNM0304